A Thing Apart

A Thing Apart

Andrew Parkin

Published by
Matador
12 Manor Walk, Coventry Road
Market Harborough
Leics LE16 9BP, UK
Tel: (+44) 1858 468828 / 469898
Fax: (+44) 1858 431649
Email: books@troubador.co.uk
Web: www.troubador.co.uk/matador

ISBN 1 899293 08 6

Cover: ER Bartlett Design

All characters in this novel are fictional and bear no intentional resemblance to any actual person living or dead.

Typesetting: Troubador Publishing Ltd, Market Harborough, UK
Printed and bound by Publish on Demand Ltd, London

Matador is an imprint of Troubador Publishing Ltd

Man's love is of a man's life a thing apart,
'Tis woman's whole existence.

Byron, *Don Juan*

When I same age as you, I ask my birth mother if true I got to die in the rite. That what other boys tell me. She look in the embers of our fire and I see water in her eyes. She say nothing. That scare me bad. I run to her sister and ask her same question. Mother Berangu always take care of me. I know she tell me truth if she can. When I ask her, she stop work on weaving her dilly bag and look at ground. She sign me squat on dirt next to her. She pass me a pile of grass for sort out and split for weaving. One time she put her arm round me, but I too big for that now. Not much hair on my face, but they all say he come proper quick. I get made into man with two other boys next day. I look at Berangu face and I see she sad, too.

"Son," she say, "I see loads of boys go to that initiation. They all come back. True you got to die, but you brought back to life, no fear." Her voice got comfort sound, spite what she say. "You know I always tell you truth. Well, truth is the All-Father send his man Thurumulan for take you. We all hear his voice in them trees and we all proper scared. Thurumulan take you and kill you and burn your body, and from the ash he make you whole again, but this time as a man, with one of your teeth out and with your foreskin gone. How he do this ... well, that magic. After, you alive as much as you are now, take my word. You know what you are as a child, but you changed for ever into a man."

My own dad squat at the fire when I get back. He pull out roo guts ready for cook. I squat next to him and try see myself as man. I look at his body, all sinew and muscle, and the bush of beard that hide half his face. He seem twice as big as me, though I reach easy to his shoulder. He don't look up but he can tell what I think because he got a lot of magic.

"Tomorrow you become a man," he say. "You get scared, but nothing scare you if you keep strong in your mind. I take you myself to Thurumulan. He know you ready. You run like emu, throw spear like man. You ready for join us men in hunt. You got to quit the company of women. When you grow wiser you learn more of our secrets. When you get good beard and know more of them secrets, I find you wife. One day you get as much magic as I got." He say all this in his stern voice, the voice he use for talk to other men. Then his voice soft, like one he use when I younger, and I know he give me comfort. "Keep in your mind, whatever happen tomorrow, Goanna look after you and keep you safe."

That night I dream Thurumulan come after me with axe in one hand and firebrand in other, but Goanna come from behind me and run up and over him. Goanna cast a spell on him and make him run away. I still scared, but this good sign.

Next day our clearing fill up with strangers from mob in next country. We call them Mairkaioo. They all painted up in red and white. They carry spears, shields and waddies for the dance. They decked out with feathers, some from the white cockatoo, some from the black cockatoo, which are the marks of their families. Most of them line up round ceremony site. Some of their elders come over where our men stand. Our men also paint themselves up for the ceremony, and my fathers paint me up. They put a stripe of white clay down my forehead to the tip of my nose. They put rings round my eyes. Then they put more stripes on my cheeks, and stripes down my arms and legs. They put sign of Goanna on my chest in red ochre. Men paint up the other two with their totems: Borrudum with Honey Ant, and Cabba with Brown Snake. They both older than me, but no taller. The strangers check the painting up all done proper right and all them right things done.

Then our fathers take us to sacred ground. All women, except our own mothers, are driven off into the bush. A ring of men from our mob stand guard with spears and waddies, make sure they don't try come back. Our fathers fit up us three boys with waist belts. We get a tail of string stuck loose in the back of each belt. Our mothers hang on to them tails, so we lead them to the sacred ground. Each boy go to his own side. I go to the side of Goanna Rock on west of our camp.

Our mothers got to lie face down behind us. They still hold our tails. Then they covered up with possum skin rugs and branches so they can't see what go on. Granddad Loolunar sing one of our songs, then men of our mob dance initiation dance. This show what boy or woman do and then what man do. Men bang with sticks on possum skins tight over knees, and tap music sticks together. The dancers show how boys and women pick berries and seeds, dig up roots, gather grubs, catch small game. They show how men hunt kangaroo and emu and do the sacred rites. Them men from that other mob watch all this. They make noises of animals and birds for help the dance. When he end their elders agree him all done proper right.

Then all that noise stop sudden. Everyone got to be quiet now. My father come over and stand by me. We all look to the bush waiting. In this quiet my mind get the idea that Thurumulan come now and kill me.

Weird noise come from trees. He get louder. He make a roar. He voice of Thurumulan, he call for boys so he can kill them. I lose control and shit myself with fear. The stink come up and I hope my father not ashamed of me. My knees feel weak. I shiver and shake, proper terrified. My father grab my arm and pull me over to the sound. As he pull me, that tail drag out of that belt. My mother know I go get killed. She wail and cry out. Them other mothers do the same. The whole clearing fill with their wails. Then those men rush about with shouts. They scatter all the women things that are around; their dilly bags and yam sticks and bowls. They hit the ground with bark and throw firebrands near them women. This make them yell out more, but they don't dare get up from ground.

The men take us to another sacred ground them women can't see. Voice of Thurumulan proper loud there. Smoky fires burn and men stamp the ground and shake their shields and spears. They kick up the dust. I start draw back but my father look near me and touch the Goanna sign he paint on my chest, and things come to my mind, and the strength of Goanna come up over me and help me

4

go on. Then Granddad Loolunar come up to me. He got most magic of anyone in our mob. He clever man, boss of ceremony. His chest and arms covered in scars. He get scar for each secret of our mob he learn. My chest got no scars.

He got his dilly bag tied to his belt. He keep The Bone in that dilly, I know.

He reach in and my stomach go crook. But he pull out a magic kooderoo shell. He sign me look inside that shell, and he make him flash in the light. Then I see he got a Rainbow Serpent inside that shell, and that Rainbow Serpent and Goanna together keep me safe.

Men go down on all fours so their backs make platform. My fathers grab me by arms and legs, lay me on that platform and hold me still. Granddad Loolunar reach into his dilly again and pull out sharp mussel shell. One of my brothers pull on skin of my cock. Loolunar slice off my hood and make me into man. He do this proper quick. I feel hot blood spill between my legs. I so worked up I don't notice pain. They drag me to fire for dry that blood and they paint that cut with white clay. They cut up my foreskin and give him to my brothers for eat. I still shocked; I don't know what go on. Before I know what happen I back on that platform and Granddad Murungunba who is tooth-doctor of our mob work on one of my teeth. Then he hook his own teeth over mine and bite him, and next he stand there with big grin and show me his own tooth-gap. He hold one of my teeth and he get me bite on wad of grass for stop blood.

My fathers and brothers go wild. They dance and throw firesticks about. That dust and smoke so thick I can't see what go on. Yawingaba call out he ready get his cock slit. Every man in our mob got to do this some time. This proper hard test. They grab Yawingaba over platform and make deep cut length of his cock, on under side. That cock almost split in two. I see blood spill out all over Yawingaba legs. That cut got to bloody hurt but he don't make any sound. He proper fired up. He stand up and show everyone the blood stream, and he let out a great roar and shake his arms in air for show what he like. I hope I brave like him when my time come. Everybody shout, and he grin at me. We both come through. Other men who slit before poke their old wounds with sharp sticks and make them bleed again. Then Yawingaba and them others dance round fire. Blood pour out over their legs. When dance over they all go to that fire and dry out their wounds.

Then Granddad Loolunar stand beside me and make me look at trees where voice of Thurumulan come. He hold out his arm towards Thurumulan and that voice stop. "Don't be scared," he say in sudden quiet. "Not true Thurumulan kill you. I tell you true story of Thurumulan. Listen careful to what I say.

"Long ago All-Father say we got to give our boys to his helper Thurumulan, so they get made into men. Thurumulan got voice like thunder. He take those boys and bring them back with tooth missing. Thurumulan say he cut those boys into pieces and burn them on fire until they nothing but ash. He say he

6

mix water with that ash and make paste put them back together again, each boy missing one tooth. But after every initiation some of them boys don't come back. Thurumulan say they get crook and die. But All-Father doubt this. He disguise himself as crow and follow next lot of novices to initiation ground.

"There he see Thurumulan bite out tooth of each boy and send them back. He don't kill them and bring them back to life. But two boys he keep behind. These boys he kill and cut into pieces and eat them. All-Father angry and call on Brown Snake bite Thurumulan and kill him dead with his poison. When Thurumulan dead, All-Father put his voice in sky. Then All-Father show clever men of our mob how we make voice of Thurumulan sound by swing bull-roarer in the trees."

The old man turn his hand a bit, and I see two of our men proper painted-up step out of the bush. They carry bull-roarers. They swing these in circles, and Thurumulan's voice come again. They got big grins. In my mind, I don't know what believe now. Granddad Loolunar tell me Thurumulan trick All-Father, but I think Granddad Loolunar trick me, and I still get killed by Thurumulan who hide in the trees. Then the old man go on:

"All-Father tell us we got to make our own initiations. We got to make voice of Thurumulan come with bull-roarers and take out tooth just like he did. All-Father tell us only men can know truth. Women got to always think Thurumulan alive."

After he say this, the old man drop his arm, and all them men around rush over with their spears held for stick in me. They point them straight at my throat and chest. I know then they trick me and they kill me after all. I fight get away, but men hold my arms. I bloody scared good. They stop with their spear points a finger away and Granddad Loolunar say in voice like thunder:

'This a secret of our mob. You tell any woman or child this secret, we all rise up and kill you! We spear you in throat. We spear you in heart. Then we spear you in liver. We cut out your eyes and feed them to the crows. We cut out your liver and feed him to the dogs. We cut out your kidneys and eat all that fat round your kidneys. We tie your body to tree and feed him to the ants and the eagles!"

I believe him, too. I know if they eat me I proper dead for ever. I look like they scare me enough, for they let go of me and I sink to ground. Granddad Loolunar give me one cut on chest, and tell me my name. Can't tell you this name, only for men of our mob. The men take back their spears and stand off. They start grin and talk among themselves, and my own dad come up to me and touch my shoulder and say in proud voice:

'Bradek, now you start life of a man."

My manhood get tested quicker than I think, for that night a great fight break out with all the men in both mobs.

At first we at peace with them Mairkaioo. They make camp a bit off from ours. They build wurlies from bark and bushes, low shelters same as ours except they don't turf theirs since they don't stay long. When night come them two mobs join together in corroboree. Our women and children come to this one; no women and children come with the other mob. That other mob bring eels they catch in a lake over their way. We got plenty of possum, bandicoot and roots. Bandicoot my favourite tucker. We build big fires and cook everything in the ash or on hot stones. Everybody excited and laugh, make jokes, dance, sing, do mad things. My own mother is Mairkaioo. A lot of that mob come to our wurly for see her. These men my relatives. One of them, Wugubu, come to me as my uncle. He pinch my arm and say, "You make a strong man." He talk funny and smell strange. "You strong because your mother Mairkaioo!" He laugh and beat his chest.

I don't like way he leave out my father. I stand up and say, "My own father is strongest man in this country!" and I beat my chest just like Wugubu do. He look down at me, not speaking, just frowning, then he give a short laugh, "Huh!" and go off.

When Sun Woman high in sky one of them Mairkaioo come in our camp. He hold a bunch of emu feathers behind his back. He shout out, "Emu run free on Goanna Rock!" This his way say our

9

mob can't catch emu. Our men chase him back to Mairkaioo camp, but he too quick, he run into middle of them Mairkaioo. They all make circle round that emu. This a great game, we all have good laugh. Our men got to wrestle with all them men round that emu. Whoever get thrown to ground got to stand out. Our men throw lots of their men to ground, but they throw more of our men to ground. In the end two of their men keep that emu safe, and only Cabba's dad on our side left. But Cabba's dad, he proper quick and strong. He jump between those two men and taunt them. They run at him, then he jump back when they close, grab their necks and bang their heads to-gether! While they dizzy he run in and wrestle that emu to ground! He grab those emu feathers and run back to our camp with them. We all give him great cheer. We shout at Mairkaioo, "Our mob stronger than Mairkaioo, emu run free all over Mairkaioo plains!" They come and wrestle our men for emu, but don't get him.

The corroboree is great. Everybody dance round the fires while Sun Woman go sleep. The men do their totem dances. The women do their sexy dances. The best bit is when the small children copy behind them men and women. Some of these children only just learn walk, but they try jump and wiggle just the same. Everybody laugh and have good time.

After a bit the dance stop. The strangers go back to their camp and I go to my camp. Now I a man, I camp with Cabba and Borrudum and other young men on one side of our mob camp. Young women camp on other side. Us men talk and joke a lot before we sleep. Some men talk a lot about them women on other side of camp. We know some of them girls want bad meet us new men. Maybe they wait out in the bush. But I go sleep. This a warm season, so I sleep outside on possum skins with no dogs. I sleep for a bit when my own father wake me and tell me get up. I see all my fathers stand there, as well as all the other men in our camp. Cabba and Borrudum there too. Some men carry long fighting spears, as well as waddies and axes. Most have throwing-sticks in the back of their belts, and they carry shields. Some have war clubs, clubs we use only in war – war club got square top and knob on the end of shaft so he can't be pulled from hand. I hear a lot of excited talk but I don't get what go on.

"What go on?" I ask Cabba.

Before Cabba can answer, his own father speak to me. "One of them Mairkaioo carry off Cabba's sister! I promise her to a man of the Guring-badawah!" He beat his chest with his shield. "I avenge this! My Giant Yam rise up and crush the man who take her!"

Cabba beat his chest and say, "My Brown Snake bite him and poison him!"

Borrudum cry out, "My Honey Ant trample him!"

I pick up my spear and shake him. "My Goanna run up over him!" All them men clap us on the back and speak up with their own vows.

We set off in a line to the other camp. Somehow

11

they know we come, for we see them pile up their fires. By time we get there, the grassland where they camp is well lit up by the fires, as well as by Moon Man who carry his torch overhead.

We make a line side by side. Our best fighters are at the front. I'm pushed to back, with Cabba and Borrudum, for we don't have shields yet, and we know enemies aim first at anyone who don't have a shield. Them Mairkaioo come in line facing us, about a spear's throw away, across the clearing. The fires blaze between us and around us. Both sides shout and rattle their spears and stamp on ground. Then our side fall quiet at a signal, and Cabba's dad step out for speak. Other side also quiet, so they hear what he say.

"Who snatch my daughter?" he call out in fierce voice. Our side all echo him. We shake our weapons. "Who take our woman?"

We see them men on other side talk among themselves. Then one of them step forward for make answer. I see, he Wugubu, my uncle. He raise his spear for quiet.

"Your daughter with me! She my wife. She come of her own wish. You don't get her back!"

Cabba's dad call back, "I promise her to a man of the Guringbadawah!"

We see some men on other side proper stopped by this, for they talk among themselves again. Big taboo, take woman promised as wife.

Wugubu answer, "Now she mine! No man take her from me! She come of her own wish!"

Cabba's dad come back talk with his brothers. After a bit, he step out again and call, "You make her go to you with sorcery! She under a spell. I fight your magic! Giant Yam fight your magic!" He already got his spear set in his spear-thrower, and now he make him fly at Wugubu, but Wugubu see him. He step aside. That spear glance off his shield. Then Wugubu fix his own spear and throw him in one quick flash. He well aimed, but Cabba's dad has eye of a hawk and speed of a lizard. He step to one side and grab that spear as he pass. A great shout go up from our side see this brave thing, for he catch spear of his enemy. We see other side upset by this. Then Cabba's dad throw Wugubu's spear back at him. Wugubu got to defend himself with his shield, and that spear land in shield with thud.

Cabba's dad run in with his war club before Wugubu can pull out spear and throw him back. Wugubu step on that spear and break him so he can use his shield, and he only just in time block first blow from war club. Wugubu got club, too, and now them two men run round each other and leap in give hits which they block with them shields. The bang and thud of their fight fill the whole place. Not long before they both got blood stream from head and shoulder where they take hits. Their fingers and thumbs all squashed when them clubs run down them shafts but they don't let go. Then Wugubu land a huge swipe full on shield of Cabba's dad and split him. Half of him fall away. Cabba's dad only left with bit which has hand-hold

13

carved in him. This proper bad for Cabba's dad, and he got to back off when Wugubu come up try finish him.

When our mob see this we all run forward and threaten Wugubu with our spears. We shout we kill him if he keep attacking. Wugubu run back to his mob, and Cabba's dad reach safety in ours. Then spears thrown from both sides, all them feller shout more and stamp more, but they don't want fight close-up. Them two sides proper even. We know all-out fight kill many men both sides.

We go on like this while Moon-Man walk from one tree-top to another. A brother of Cabba's dad take spear in his thigh, but we can pull him out and he live. We run out to skim our throwing sticks into their line and these catch a lot of men. We give them bruises or broken legs. We see two men laid out on the other side; how bad hurt we don't know. When everybody know we in a stand-off, we pack up and go back to our place. My first battle is over! He scary with them weapons flying and all that, but not half as scary as Thurumulan when he make me man.

I don't do much, but I feel proper tired when we get back. I fall asleep soon as I lie down for rest. When I wake up, Sun Woman already get up and I know something exciting go on. Men and women run past our family fire to the side of our camp. I jump up, grab my spear and join them. Everybody in our mob jump and shout madly. Then I see Cabba's dad in the middle of this crowd. He hold a roo skin full of something. Behind him his daughter stand.

She keep her eyes on ground. Cabba's dad shout and jump and beat his chest. "I kill Wugubu!" he call out. "I creep to his wurly in the night and spear him! My spear pass through his body and pin him to the ground. My Giant Yam overcome him. Now my daughter free of his spell!" A great cheer go up, but Cabba's dad not finished. "I cut off his legs and arms! See!" He let go the rug and Wugubu's arms and legs fall out on ground. We all go wild with excitement and cheering. People leap about, they dance and stamp. Cabba's dad pick up them bits of Wugubu and cover them with hot ashes of his family fire. When they cooked, we all eat Wugubu and we know he never trouble us again. We smear his grease on our children for protect them. Cabba's dad is avenged.

Them Mairkaioo go. They don't attack us in our camp, for our women are good fighters with digging stick and spear and our men and women together are twice as many as them. They go back to their own country.

We in this camp some time. Food get short. Women got to walk long way for dig up root and pick fruit and seed. Then we see smoke signal from the plains down the valley. This come from our hunters. We fix up these signals ahead of time. Two grey columns say plenty kangaroo there. One black column with gaps say they need help trap them.

We know this trap well; we use him before. All men

15

still in camp set out for join hunt. First we cover our bodies with mud so our smell don't reach kangaroo. We carry firesticks and hunting spears and waddies. We creep down past the animals which eat the grass in that plain. Them kangaroo many like fingers on two hands. We keep well off, out of sight behind bushes. Our dogs know keep out of sight too. We make no noise; our hands do all the talking to man or dog.

We reach the men who make that smoke. Someone sign for us spread out in wide line upwind of them kangaroo. This risky for they might smell us, but we got to cut off their escape across the plains and head them into valley. We creep into line across plain, well below kangaroo. Through tuft of grass I see them a long way off. They stand up with ears cocked. They know something wrong. They ready run. Maybe they smell them dogs. Then I get sign from man on my left fire grass. I pass this sign to man on my right, and plunge my firestick into clump of grass. He flare up as the dry ends catch, then die back. Not much wind that day, but enough make that flame spread to next clump – and so fire go on, jump from clump to clump. Sometimes we got to refire him when he die out. I see great line of fire and smoke going on, and through gap in smoke I see them kangaroo start up and hop away up the valley. We go on with smoke; our ring of men and dogs all time close round neck of that valley. Dense bush cover sides of that valley and top got rocks and boulders. Those plains kangaroo don't like that kind of country. They try keep in the grass while we come all time closer. We send our dogs chase any of those kangaroo that try break out. Them dogs drive those kangaroo back. Them dingoes good hunters, they get their share of the kill.

Many small animals run out of fire – bandicoots, goannas, snakes. These we hit with our waddies as they pass. I hit two snakes and a bandicoot and stick them in my waist string for carry them. I don't catch them goannas because I Goanna myself. Then we right up on them kangaroo and they got to make their last try jump out of fire circle. Now we throw our spears and bring them down. I don't get a throw in, but I find a roo down near me and finish him off with my waddy. Then ring of men all come together, and we see we kill all the kangaroos. We raise our hands in joy, and shout and dance at this great success.

Back at camp, we gut them roos and cut off their feet so we can take out their sinews, which are good for tie axe head and bind spear. Now I man I got to make proper spear for fight, and got to get axe and shield by and by. Then we cover them kangaroo whole with hot ash for cook them. Nearly every family in our mob get a kangaroo. Not often we see so much meat. This a great day and we dance and sing lots more for celebrate him. When them roos are cooked they handed out as got to by law. Our grandfathers choose first. They ask for tail, which is best bit, but if they feel generous they might pass that up and let someone else have a go. Then fathers and uncles and brothers choose their bits, then women and children. Hunters always got to choose last. Today I'm a hunter and I got to choose last. This no problem, we got plenty meat go round and we all have a feast. I proud choose last now I man.

After some days we start pack up our camp move on. The women got to carry all the kit and rugs and things, as well as their babies, and we help load them up. They put woman tucker for journey and other small things in dilly bag that hang down back and tied round forehead. They carry baby on neck. Baby got to hold on to mother's hair. If he don't, he fall off! This leave mother hands free for carry bowls or skin and yam stick and pick fruit and seed on journey. Us men carry our weapons so we can hunt on the move and keep women safe.

When them women move off, my own dad come up to me and tell me go with two other feller in our mob who are Goannas. One of them is uncle Yawingaba. The other is grandfather called Moyana. They come over to me. They all painted up with Goanna signs, same as me, for mine don't wear off yet spite that mud. That mud fall off easy when he dry out. They sign for me follow them, and I know they show me Goanna secrets now I man.

We go over to Goanna Rock. I Goanna because I born near this rock. When babies born the spirit of the place that live there since Dreamtime go into their bodies. But I never go up to that rock before, because him a sacred place and children don't go near sacred place. A child see a sacred place, he die proper dead because he can't stand that magic. Now I man I can stand that magic. We go through the bush and climb the hill to Goanna Rock. Top of that hill bare apart from crooked white gum and big grey rock. Yawingaba go off with Moyana. They tell me wait at that rock. By and by they come back. Moyana carry bark board covered with painting. I see there are circles on him joined by lines of dots. Then Moyana sign me squat and he talk to me.

"Now you man you got to come to this place every year. Maybe two, three times every year. Goanna Rock your Dreaming." He hold out his hand to north. "In Dreamtime Goanna come down from that way. He travel long time until he reach this place. He rest in shade of that gum tree. Here he turn himself into stone, claim this place for all his descendants like you and me. Now, look over there at that rock. See that hole at front? That Goanna's mouth. See that bulge on top? That Goanna's eye. Down there, near the ground, those bits are Goanna's legs and tail."

As he point out these things, I see him true that rock is Goanna, and I see his mouth and his eye and his legs and his tail. Just then a goanna scuttle out on top of that rock. He stop still when he spot us, and cock his head to look one eye on me. Moyana smile and nod. This goanna just like the rock. I know Moyana's magic bring out this goanna. Then Moyana hold up that board.

"This board of Goanna Dreaming. This sacred board. We hide him in sacred place. Today I show that place to Yawingaba. When you got your cock slit, we show you this place.

"This board show journey of Goanna from north."
He point to the circles. "These them waters Goanna
drink on journey. This one river near Goanna Rock.
This one lake we walk to now." He tell me about all
them waters on that board, and then say, "You got
to learn all them waters on this board and all them
tracks in between. Now, I go with Yawingaba put
him back. You don't follow. You see hiding place
before you ready, a *mamu* kill you."

I stay there until they come back, for I know *mamu*
watch that place.

We soon catch up with the women. I
see Cabba's sister. She proper quiet.
Her mother walk alongside her.
When I pass I see her back burnt. I
catch up with Cabba and ask him how his sister
burn her back. He say his dad hold her over fire
drive out spell of Wugubu and teach her not run off
again.

We walk many days. Some rain fall on the way and
sometimes we got to shelter in caves. When no
caves, we get proper cold on the plains. We got
trouble keep our firesticks burning. Leaders fire
grass so we can see which way we got to go.
Yawingaba show me how tell water from Goanna
board. Each stream or billabong we come to, he
take me all round that place, show him to me from
all sides. I got to remember what he look like from
all sides.

By and by we come near water at north of Goanna board. This place belong Guringbadawah mob. We set fire to grass as we come near, so Guringbadawah know we come in peace. Enemy come proper stealthy, hide, don't fire grass. Then in sky we see big column of black smoke. He go straight up very high then spread out at top. All our mob excited by this, for he mean Guringbadawah got plenty tucker and want us join feast.

We hurry over last bit and soon come to lake side. He big lake but not deep, plenty land flooded by rain, plenty island in lake. First thing we see him full of tucker. Swan, spoonbill, egret, duck, heron – every type of bird like water. Now rain finish, them birds make nest, lay eggs. Round lake side we see camp of Guringbadawah. We got to talk with Guringbadawah before we take any tucker belong them. Granddad Loolunar and other clever men from our mob go round their way with clenched fists raised. Clenched fist say "we hold firestick, come as friend". They take gifts of woman tucker, axe heads and possum skin rugs. Guringbadawah say they got plenty tucker and water for everyone and tell us come to big corroboree that night.

We stay long time that place. Plenty tucker and good corroborees. We wade out to islands, collect plenty eggs. Women collect plenty lily root in that lake. We hunt birds easy. We send women out in lake. They crouch low, wear grass or branch on head so look like plant float on water. They walk out behind birds. Men wait on shore. Then women all stand up same time and shout. Birds fly up quick towards us. Great many birds, block out sky like dark cloud. We throw our sticks into cloud of birds. Nearly every stick hit a bird, bring him down. Plenty fish in that lake too. We make fish spears and stick them fish by wade out or from bark canoe. Every day we get big feast.

Cabba's sister get better after her burns. The spirit of that lake go in her and make a baby inside her. Cabba's dad give her to that Guringbadawah man she promised to. Guringbadawah man cut her hair for make good string. All wife hair belong husband. She proper good wife with baby come by and by. Her husband give Cabba's dad black stone axe head. This black stone hardest we know. We never see stone like that down our way. Guringbadawah say they get stone from mob further north. Cabba's dad fix axe in haft with dry roo dung and gum resin heated in fire, then bind him up with roo sinew. Everybody have a go with axe belong Cabba's dad. I follow honey bee back to nest in hollow tree, then use axe get at nest. That honey sweet, proper good tucker.

Birds start get less, we got to hunt on land. One day Guringbadawah hunters come back from hunt after emu. They go many days. Some big noise in their camp, we go over hear what they say. They say they don't see emu. They see big beast with two heads travel across plain far to east. They keep out of sight. Beast too big for hunt. Their party too small attack animal that big. They follow beast. He wander off out of their country into country to north. Then they come back.

Cabba's dad say, 'My Giant Yam rise up and crush

that beast!"

Cabba say, "My Brown Snake bite him and poison him!"

Borrudum say, "My Honey Ant trample him!"

I say, "My Goanna run up over him!"

Us new men have proper good spear now. We shake them. Cabba's dad shake his axe and show how he bury him in that beast. We set off in big party kill beast with two heads.

Four days we travel east before we come to tracks of that beast in sandy patch. This new country for our mob. We never see tracks like that. They same tracks seen by Guringbadawah hunters before. They old tracks, but we can see beast got legs number of two beasts, and two tails. Them two tails very heavy, they drag in ground behind beast, make deep furrow. Beast very heavy, too: his footprint four times more deep than footprint belong man. We never see footprint like that before. That beast got no toes.

We follow trail two days, but don't see beast. He travel straight over plain without wander off here or there. We see he eat grass. Sometimes pull up by root. We find piles of his dung. We never see dung like that before. Size of pile show he big beast, big like Goanna Rock. But we don't see beast.

Cabba's dad say he sense another mob nearby. We go careful, keep hidden in case they not friend. We don't make smoke this trip. Other mob don't make smoke. Guringbadawah say land beyond tracks belong another mob. We camp and wait.

By and by Cabba's dad say he see man of strange mob on rock across gully. He go over with clever man of Guringbadawah talk to stranger. They go long time. When come back, Cabba's dad tell us what they talk about.

'Strangers say they see beast with two heads cross their country, then go north. They say they see man sit on that beast. They say that man got no body."

"What you mean?" we all ask. "He got no body?"

Cabba's dad show with his hand he don't know. "That what other mob say. That man got no body. They say they all scared. That man, that beast, they spirit from Dreamtime. That other mob all hide when he go by."

I think man with no body more scary than man with body. We all ask what we do now. Cabba's dad most clever man there, he decide.

"This magic too strong," he say. "We got to go back to lake, ask Granddad Loolunar. He say what we do."

Granddad Loolunar say beast with two heads and man with no body bloody bad for our mob. He sing them away, they not come back. He go to edge of our camp, side towards beast with two heads and man with no body. He sing them proper good and point them so they don't come back.

Four times more we make that journey each time Sun-Woman tire of climb so high in sky. Four times more we go to lake. Four times more we camp near Goanna Rock. I grow beard, learn some secrets, get a few scars. One time I get my cock slit when my brother go through initiation, like Yawingaba do with me. I don't cry out, I show I man. We don't see beast with two heads or man with no body. Magic of Granddad Loolunar proper strong. Then, when we camp near Goanna Rock, Granddad Loolunar get crook and die.

"Who kill Granddad Loolunar?" we ask Cabba's dad. Cabba's dad now cleverest man in our mob. He got scars like Granddad Loolunar. Granddad Loolunar give him dilly bag when he die.

Now Cabba's dad got The Bone.

Cabba's dad search ground near Loolunar body. He find cut blade of grass near body. He find stone near body. When press stone on ground, make print like that print with no toes. He see small green lizard near body. Lizard run away into rocks.

"Two-head beast kill Loolunar," say Cabba's dad. "This the grass two-head beast eat. This the footprint of two-head beast. Two-head beast turn himself into green lizard so we don't see him, then run away."

We don't like this. If man kill Loolunar, we know what do. We kill man. If two-head beast kill Loolunar, then turn into lizard, we can't catch lizard. We look out for green lizard everywhere in that camp,

25

see many, kill a few, but don't know if we kill right green lizard.

Cabba's dad call on Giant Yam rise up and crush beast with two heads. Then he take The Bone and point in direction of tracks we find in stranger country. Hair cord tied to that Bone go round arm belong Cabba's dad, get strength from his blood. Other hair cord tied to that Bone go round arm of Murungunba, brother of dead man. Strength from his blood go into Bone too. Them two men sing secret song that make bone fly into heart and kill dead that beast with two heads.

We put Granddad Loolunar's body in tree, cover him over with logs so eagle don't eat him. At night we have big meeting for mourn Loolunar. He got two wives. They proper sad. They hit their heads with stones, make plenty blood. They make mud cap on hair, got to wear until Loolunar spirit rest. Them women taken over as wife by Murungunba. Brother always take wife when man die. We can't say name of Loolunar for long time, till we don't see his footprints in camp and his spirit rest. We say name of dead man, his spirit think we call him, he don't rest. His spirit come to us angry, maybe kill us for call him. Can say that name now, for long time back. Loolunar great man, take long time rest his spirit. We come back finish bury Loolunar when flesh leave his body. Then come back many year, make ceremony rest his spirit until all done proper.

Next time we near lake, Cabba's dad take us out to stranger country in east again. We see beast with two heads dead in plain. We watch long time from rocks, make sure he don't move. But he proper dead, don't move all day. We go out to beast with two heads. Never see beast like that before. All flesh gone, heads gone away. Got two backbones made of wood. All skeleton left made of wood. He got bits of skin like paperbark. He got two lots of ribs like starfish in circle. Belly of that beast big like cave. Cabba's dad go right inside belly. We keep out, scared beast eat Cabba's dad. Then he come out.

"This beast proper dead," he say. "That Bone kill him proper dead. Spirit of Loolunar avenged!"

White dust cover his hands, like ground seed for damper but proper small, fine like bulldust. He say he find dust in dilly bag inside belly of beast. We taste dust. He not bad, taste like tucker.

Next time we camp near Goanna Rock, we take down bones of Loolunar. We bury them bones and make proper good ceremony. After, my own dad come over to me and speak to me.

He say, "Bradek, now you got beard and you got some scars on your chest, I find you wife. I find you Mairkaioo wife like your mother. Tomorrow you go meet your mother-in-law."

That fight with Mairkaioo long time back. Our mob and their mob make many marriage: no fight last long. Now I go with my own father and his brothers and my own mother and Berangu meet my mother-in-law. My own mother White Cockatoo so I got to take Black Cockatoo for wife.

We sit near fire of father belong my mother-in-law. His name Yarrungaitj. We wait quiet. Soon Yarrungaitj come. He got plenty scars. He sit with my father. Behind Yarrangaitj sit husband belong my mother-in-law and others from their mob. Husband old man like Yarrungaitj. My father look at fire and speak to Yarrangaitj. Yarrangaitj look at fire and speak to my father. My father give Yarrangaitj present of fine spear head and rare shell. My father put them present on ground between them. Yarrangaitj pick up. He look close at present, take and show to others with him. They talk with my father, then my father say to me:

"Bradek, Yarrungaitj say you can have Black Cockatoo for wife. Your mother-in-law name Jinggaya. Yarrungaitj promise her next born daughter be your wife. When that child grow to age, she come live with you. Now, Jinggaya come and you see her for only time."

Now, I know what you think. You think I full grown man, how can I wait without woman until this daughter born and grow up. I normal man, I got plenty juice in my cock like other men. My juice shoot up higher than a tall man. Some women in my mob want sex with me, get my juice. Them women, they wife belong other man, or promised for wife, so taboo sex with me unless husband say can. Murungunba, he now got four wives. He old man, he have hard time look after one woman. Them four wives young women. Plenty more women in our mob like that. Plenty time we go in secret into bush. Every feller know this. No one complain, they all do same. But we got to make sure no one find out too.

I know I see Jinggaya once only, for law say man don't look at mother-in-law and woman don't look at son-in-law after marriage fixed. When woman mother-in-law all her sisters got to look out and warn her if her son-in-law come near. Then she go hide in bush.

Jinggaya come very slow to fire place, her head hang down. She proper shy. Her father speak to her and she look at me quick. That look … oh! I never see woman look my way like that before. She good looking woman. She young age like me. She got good skin, round belly. She got hair fair like child. Her hair good and long, make proper good string. She wear parrot feathers on string round neck, red, blue, green, yellow and she got feather from black cockatoo and white cockatoo as well. Her body strong, she carry plenty, she dig plenty yam. Her breasts keep baby plenty full. Her backside stand out proud. I look at her, glad she my mother-in-law so I can have wife like her by and by. My father say to Yarrungaitj, "This good mother-in-law for my son."

Yarrungaitj say to Jinggaya, "Now you got son-in-law you don't look at him. You look at your son-in-law, you get killed." Then her father send her away. She take quick look near me before she go. I see smile in her eyes. That smile like Sun Woman come from behind cloud, make me feel warm. Then she turn and go. She leave only footprint in dirt. I look long time at that footprint. I see where foot arch, where toes come together, where side of foot run. That footprint of strong woman who walk smooth.

My father see me look at footprint. He look at my face. I look away. My father say, "Now you got wife you don't look at your mother-in-law. You look at your mother-in-law, you get killed."

When we leave that camp, I walk through soft ground, leave my footprint for Jinggaya. Why I do this, I not sure.

That night I lie on roo skin by fire. I look in fire. I look at flames go up, go down. I see wind breathe on embers, make grey ember go red then grey again. Stick break and fall down in fire. Yellow sparks fly up, taken away by wind. I think, that wind, he come from over Mairkaioo way. Mother Berangu sit near me and say, "Why you look sad, Bradek? Why you quiet? You got to be happy now you get fine wife."

I keep look at fire. She right, I sad. Berangu always good friend for me. I glad she ask, but I can't answer. I don't know answer. She stay long time by fire. After long time, I say, "Mother Berangu, you proper kind, you good mother. I don't know why I quiet. I feel I got to be quiet, that all."

She touch my arm and don't say more.

At first light I sit mend spear by fire. Cabba come and sit near. I don't look at him, I fix spear careful. After a bit, Cabba say, "You proper quiet, Bradek.

30

You crook?"

I carry on fix spear. "You right, Cabba. I quiet. Maybe crook, maybe not. Maybe need quiet day." He go.

Later Borrudum come sit near fire. He say, "Cabba say he think you crook. You come hunt with us?"

I look at fire. I don't want look at Borrudum. I say, "No, I feel like I hunt alone today. You go hunt with Cabba. I need quiet day – get used to being married man!" Borrudum laugh at my joke. I get wife before him or Cabba. They want wife too. I get wife, not sure if I want.

I go hunt. I pick up spears, go across plain, over Mairkaioo way. My own mother Mairkaioo, I can hunt Mairkaioo country but plenty of our mob can't follow. I go stealthy, don't make smoke so kangaroo don't see. I don't see kangaroo. I go quiet, rock to rock, tree to tree. See no kangaroo, see no Mairkaioo except where they make smoke out on plain. I near Mairkaioo camp. All quiet near their camp. Men go hunt, women gather tucker. I go near soft ground where I leave my footprint. I hide behind rock, make sure no one near. Then I go down and look at my footprint.

I see another footprint inside my footprint. That other footprint small. I see toes gather together - woman toes. I see where side of foot run, where he curve in from ball. I know that footprint. Mix them footprints taboo. I kick dust over footprints, run back to my camp. Someone put spell on me.

We go again to lake in Guring-badawah country. We come back to Goanna Rock. Moyana and Yawingaba show me cave where sacred Goanna board hide. Moyana show me how repaint Goanna sign at back of Goanna Rock. Moyana show me how cut bark for painting, how dry him, how make paint out of ochres and egg yolk and other stuff. Then he start show me how paint Goanna Dreaming pictures which tell sacred story of all us Goannas.

We hold another ceremony keep spirit of Loolunar in peace. Cabba's dad teach me funeral song. I learn this good, get another scar. I get plenty scars. Then one evening Cabba's dad call me, he say, "Bradek, get spear. We go hunt kangaroo."

I get spear, go off with Cabba's dad. But he don't take me to hunting grounds. He take me to secret place, where plenty sign say to all feller of our mob keep away, this place a taboo place. No one go there that I ever see. In this place many stone sit in a circle. Cabba's dad tell me why this circle sacred. He ask me if anything trouble me.

My mind go to Jinggaya. That spell trouble me. But I don't want tell Cabba's dad about spell. I say to him, "Uncle, I know the All-Father cover the earth with plants we eat and plants the kangaroo and the emu eat. Why he send so many insect eat those plants too so we get less?"

Cabba's dad proper quiet long time. He look at my face. I think he look inside my head. I afraid he know this not my real trouble. Then he speak slow and careful.

'True All-Father cover the land with all kind of tree and plant and grass and he put berry on the tree and root on the plant and seed on the grass so we get plenty tucker. Them trees the most perfect trees, grow tall and strong with sweet berry. Them plants the most perfect plants, grow tasty shoot and root. That grass the most perfect grass, sway in the wind and ripen good seed. When the land all covered, All-Father sit down and look at all his work and think, I make best world for men live in. But while he think this, *mamu* come and see what he make; they see his trees and his plants and his grass and they see them perfect and they get jealous. They got nothing that good in world of them *mamu*. In secret them *mamu* decide they destroy all that work of All-Father. Them *mamu* send ants eat them trees, and caterpillars eat them plants, and weevils eat that grass. The world covered in insects and they eat up all the tucker. All-Father see that all the tucker nearly gone and he ask Nungeena for help since she mother of natural things. Nungeena send echidna eat them ants and small birds eat them caterpillars and weevils. And that what happen now. That echidna eat them ants and them small birds eat them caterpillars and them weevils so still enough tucker left for men."

When he finish he look through me again and he put his thought in my head without say words. His thought say, I know this not what trouble you. I answer your question because him a good question, but he not what trouble you. I don't force you tell

33

me what trouble you. When you ready, you tell.

Then he say with words, 'I bring you here tell you about spirits. This place here good for spirits, this a sacred place. He all link to spirit land. You know your *yowi*, that your soul, that who you are. Your *yowi* keep inside your body while you alive. When you dead, your *yowi* go out to land of *dowi*, where spirits live, and he live there same he live here while you alive. While you alive, your *mulowil* keep your *yowi* inside your body. That *mulowil*, he like stone in quandong, that *yowi*, he like kernel inside that stone. That stone he keep in that kernel proper good until quandong fall from tree. That *dowi* he like fruit and leaves wrap round stone in layers and like wind and smoke outside them leaves. You got five layer of *dowi* outside your *mulowil*, then two more. Each layer of that *dowi* for different kind of spirit.'

I listen proper hard to Cabba's dad. When he tell me about them spirits, he look at me with strong eye. I can't look any place but in his eyes. I see he proper serious and he tell me big secret. I think hard about my *yowi* inside my *mulowil* and about all that *dowi* outside.

Then Cabba's dad say, 'I learn from your grandfather just died how take my *yowi* out of that *mulowil* while I still alive. My *yowi* travel all over that *dowi*. So do yours if you learn how. My *yowi* visit all them spirit in the *dowi*. My *yowi* visit spirit of seasons, ask them help bring rain. My *yowi* visit spirit of plants and trees, ask them grow good root and berry for us eat. My *yowi* visit spirit of our ancestors, ask for

34

any advice help our mob. My *yowi* travel through that *dowi* and visit your *yowi* any time."

This when I see how Cabba's dad clever man, why he got so much magic. He got his own magic and he got the magic of all them spirit too. I ask him, "Uncle, how do I learn travel in that *dowi* and visit all them spirit?"

He answer, "This not hard. You got to learn how get your *yowi* through that *mulowil*. When your *yowi* get through, he free roam anywhere. All you got to do is think your *yowi* out of that *mulowil*. But him not ordinary thinking. You got to learn powerful thinking, think with whole body, think with all feeling you got. When you think like that and your *yowi* start roam, your body on this earth like asleep. I teach you this thinking. We come to this place again, I teach you good powerful thinking."

When I get back to young man camp, my own dad there. He call me over and say, "Bradek, I come from Yarrungaitj. He say Jinggaya have baby daughter while we up at lake. This daughter fine baby. Now you got proper good wife!" He clap his hands and laugh.

I try look happy but can't speak. I force smile at my dad and he get on with his things. But when he don't see, I don't smile. I feel strange. I feel crook. I happy I got wife, I think. Good get wife, every feller want get wife. But when my dad say Jinggaya name, my hair stand up and my skin shiver. I see that look she give me, I see her smile and I see that fair hair. I see her footprint in mine. When my dad say Jinggaya name, all that spell come back and I don't feel good. I go in bush alone, sit by creek, watch water, try shake off that spell, but he come back proper strong. I think I die from that spell. I need help, but who help me?

I stay in bush until dark, come back for sleep. Can't sleep, too much trouble. Need help. How get help? Then I think, I Goanna, spirit of Goanna help me. I think what Cabba's dad say. Spirit of Goanna in *dowi*. I need find spirit of Goanna proper bad. I think about my *yowi* proper hard, think about push him through that *mulowil*. I lie on possum skin. I got my eyes shut. All that camp quiet. I think so hard don't hear frogs call any more. Don't hear mopoke call. Don't hear anything. I think fierce push my *yowi* through that *mulowil*, find spirit of Goanna. I *got* to find Goanna. I think this with all my strength. I *got* to find Goanna.

I feel my mind go out into dark place. All dark, like night when Moon Man don't come. All empty. But that place not cold, feel like something live in that place. I think, is this my *yowi* reach that *dowi*? I don't know, maybe I just imagine. But my mind *somewhere*, and that not normal place. I need find Goanna. And when I think this, I see Goanna in that dark place. He start small then get bigger. He giant Goanna, he stand on two legs and he show me his pale belly covered with dark spots. His two big eyes look at me. I see all them brown and green scales round his nose gleam, and his big eyes look at me. He don't say anything, but he flick out his tongue and I see his tongue forked and his big black eyes look at me.

36

"Goanna!" I call out. "I need your help!" He keep those eyes on me and flick out his tongue again. I know he want me tell him my trouble. "I – I under a spell. Someone put a spell on me." Goanna still say nothing and I know I got to tell him more. "This spell, he make me think about Jinggaya like .. like no other woman. I can't help think about her and I feel sick from think about her. I think about her like I want her as wife. But I got a wife, and that wife Jinggaya's daughter, and Jinggaya my mother-in-law and everyone know taboo see mother-in-law …"

I know I don't tell this proper good to Goanna, for I bad troubled, but I see some different look come in his eye. His head go to one side a bit, and then I see that Goanna understand me, he understand me proper good. His look say, I understand your trouble, and I want help you. I happy I tell Goanna and he want help me, and I feel a warm feeling come all over. I know Goanna can help me. But when Goanna open his mouth for speak and tell me what I got to do, he disappear all quick. He not there, that place all dark except for small man far away. This man get bigger and nearer and come right up close. When I see his face, I see him Cabba's dad. I feel hair rise on back of neck.

"Bradek," he say. His voice like voice of Thurumulan. "I come warn you. This proper bad what you think about Jinggaya. This all wrong, this against the law of our mob. You got to forget about Jinggaya, you got to want her daughter instead. You see Jinggaya, we all kill you. You see Jinggaya, I kill you myself." Then I see he got spear and he shake

37

him at me. Then he go and I left shaking and feel cold.

When morning come I proper crook. I don't want see anybody, don't want stay in camp. I go bush, keep out of sight. But on way Cabba's dad step out in front of me, stop me going.

'Oh, Uncle,' I say. I shocked. I don't expect see him. 'Oh, Uncle, you come to me in the night ...'

'Yes, Bradek,' he say. 'My *yowi* come to you in the night. I know you troubled. My *yowi* come make sure you well.'

'I feel good now, Uncle,' I say. I tell lie. 'I do as you say.' I tell lie again. 'Now I go hunt far off.' I don't know I tell lie again, but I do.

Cabba's dad look at me. He say, 'When you come back, I show you how travel in *dowi*.'

'Yes, Uncle,' I say, and run off into bush.

You think I wander anywhere in bush but I tell you truth, I go like flight of spear into Mairkaioo country. That spell, he pull me like fish hooked on line. I know I got to see Jinggaya, know what she do. I go to Mairkaioo open country, see smoke where women gather food far off. I hide behind grass, behind tree, behind rock so get near and they don't see me. When I near, I see fair hair of Jinggaya proper good. She in tall grass, she pick millet. Far off, I see big pile of millet stalks them women build for sun make dry. Seed fall out easy when that millet dry. In clear patch nearby I see baby on ground. Baby pick up stones, put in mouth. Baby happy. Jinggaya happy. She sing a little, call out to other women. Them other women got baby on ground too. Them women all call one another, say how good seed, talk about grind seed make damper, say how happy baby, talk about how baby grow, call out make jokes all time. I creep up proper quiet, spy on Jinggaya from behind bush, like hunt kangaroo. When I close, I catch her scent. Her scent sweet. I see her stop, look all about like she know someone there. I stop breath, keep still. She don't see me, she start pick again. I see her. I see her proper close. I see her fair hair, I see her skin, I see them small light hairs on her skin. I see her eyes, I see her lips. I see her eyebrows, I see her chin, I see her cheeks. I see her fingers, I see her feet, I see every part of that woman. I see her nature, she got a happy nature, she laugh and joke all time. That Jinggaya the most beautiful woman ever come to this earth. That spell not a bad spell, that spell bring me to most beautiful woman on this earth.

I can't help him, I step from behind bush, show myself. She see me quick, look shocked. She drop millet with small cry. She run to baby, pick up quick and run off to other women. She call out. I frighten her proper bad. I stupid. I most stupid man ever come to this earth. I run away from that place like startled emu, I blunder through bushes, get scratch all over, I run and run until can run no more, then lie in bush panting. I think, Bradek, you most stupid man ever come to this earth.

I don't sleep that night. I angry. I afraid Cabba's dad come while I sleep, get in my mind again. I sorry frighten Jinggaya. I sad lose her. I rest against tree, lie in grass, bad troubled. In morning I don't want go back to our mob. I wander to millet country, way I come, follow my own track through bush. When I near millet country, I stop dead. All that skin on back of neck go cold, he walk up and down my shoulders, my hair stand up. I don't believe what I see. There, in sandy patch, is one of them footprint I leave when I run from millet country. And inside that footprint is another footprint. This small footprint, with woman's toes. I know that footprint. I know that footprint belong Jinggaya. I look all about good, in case anyone watch. But no one there. I all alone. I go up close, stand right over footprint, then squat alongside him. I watch footprint belong Jinggaya long time in case he magic footprint and he disappear. But he don't disappear. I go away short time, then come back. He still there. That real footprint. That footprint made by Jinggaya. She give me sign.

I know I crook now, for I hear my heart in my ears. He go bang, bang, bang. I know I got to go all way to millet country, find Jinggaya again. My heart he go bang bang so loud I afraid all bush hear him. But I go all way to millet country again, proper secret same like last time. I get on high ground, see all over that grass country. I see them women again all spread out in different place pick millet. I see one woman long way from others. She pick millet near where bush start. She got fair hair. She got baby on neck. That woman Jinggaya. I know she choose place where I can meet her in secret. I see her look all about while she pick. As she pick she walk further from other women, closer to bush. She look all about for me.

I stalk round to bush near Jinggaya. I know she sense me, for she look all time my way. I look through fork in tree, see her smile my way. I remember that smile, he make me warm all over. Then I step out. She hold big bunch of millet stalks to breast like baby. She look shy. She look at ground, then at me, then ground again. I open my mouth say "Jinggaya," but no word come. That spell stop me speak. She take step back, I afraid she run off again. She look over shoulder, make sure no other woman see. Then she look at me and she smile.

"Bradek," she say with smile. "You not allowed here." She say this quiet, so other women don't hear.

What she say true, but she don't go away. I answer, "You not allowed here too."

She keep look at me. I keep look at her. We both smile. I see her hair close, see him not as fair as I remember, him got dark streaks. Then she say, "I happy see you."

I say, "I happy see you, Jinggaya."

Then she look over her shoulder again, look troubled. "I got to go now," she say.

"You come here tomorrow?" I ask. She look at me and I see her eyes say "Yes". Then she turn and walk off with baby and millet toward other women.

That night I sleep in young man's camp. They ask where I go. I say I chase kangaroo over Mairkaioo way. Cabba say, "What colour hair kangaroo got?" I think he don't believe me. But I too excited, I don't care. I happy. I have plenty dream about Jinggaya that night. I got so many dreams in my mind nothing can reach my *yowi*. That good spell keep out Cabba's dad.

Next morning before Sun Woman get up I go quiet out of camp and over Mairkaioo way. I already wait in trees near millet country when them women come and spread out for pick millet. I see Jinggaya come straight to my trees. She look over shoulder, make sure other women don't see, then walk into bush. I call soft, "Jinggaya," but she already know I there. She come up quiet, give smile. She not shy this time. Her finger tip touch my arm proper soft. She sign me squat on ground, out of sight of women in field. I squat. She lift baby off neck, put on ground, then she squat too. She look at me and smile again. I too happy for talk. I sit there, say nothing, smile like stupid feller.

She reach in dilly bag and pull out damper and berries. She give this to me. I take and eat, for I proper hungry. I happy eat Jinggaya food.

Jinggaya play with baby a bit. I say, "What baby name?"

She say, "This baby name Monanggu."

I say, "Monanggu," and touch baby cheek. Baby laugh.

Jinggaya smile at me and say, "My father say this baby your wife." She smile all time. I not sure what she tell me. I look at her with question in eyes. She carry on smile at me. Then she say, "I don't think this baby your wife." I say nothing, I not sure. Then she say, "Sun Woman up high. I got to pick millet." She get up quick.

"Tomorrow you come again?" I ask.

She smile as she walk off and again I see her eyes say "Yes".

On way back I see tree hole make good possum nest. I make toe step in tree with axe, right foot, left foot, right foot, climb that tree proper quick. I break into hole with my axe, catch big possum. I glad I got tucker show when I back in camp.

Next day Jinggaya ask me about my family. I tell her my own dad and own mum good to me, and Mother Berangu spoil me. She say her own father tell her about my mother and her sister Berangu. Everybody like Berangu, she happy person, make everybody laugh, she kind person, she look after everybody. She come to my mob same time my mother, my mother become wife my father, Berangu become wife brother belong my father. Then brother belong my father get killed dead in fight. Berangu come live with my father and her sister.

'So your father got two wives? No more?" she say.

'No, no more," I say.

'Like you," she say, with small laugh.

I troubled. 'How you mean, like me?" That small laugh become big laugh. She roll on ground and laugh loud. 'How you mean?" I say again.

'Hah! You got two wives! You got me and you got baby Monanggu!" She laugh like mad. Before I can ask her what she mean, she pick up baby and run back to other women.

That night I think about what she say. I know him true I want Jinggaya for wife. And him true Yarrun-gaitj give me Monanggu for wife. Maybe Jinggaya tell me she want be my wife. So maybe I got two wives. But feller can't have mother and daughter for wife. I sleep troubled think about this. In morning I glad Cabba's dad don't visit my *yowi* that night, or he angry enough kill me dead.

In young man camp they tease me, say I don't hunt kangaroo but hunt for woman. I don't tell them they wrong - they don't believe me if I do. I tell them they jealous. I don't think they know who I go see. I not sure they my friend if they find out. I think Cabba maybe guess I see Jinggaya, but he say nothing. I tell him nothing, for if Cabba know truth for sure he can't be my friend and good son same time.

Next day I ask Jinggaya about her family. She say her husband bad man. He beat her when she don't work hard enough gather tucker. He got bad temper, always pick fight with other men. Her father good man, but believe strong in law, he don't let her leave her husband. She say other women good to her, help protect her, but each night she fear go back to husband.

Then she say, "Will you be my husband, Bradek?"

I say, "What you mean? You got husband."

"I want leave that bad man. I want you for husband. I want make new life with you."

I say, "I take you for wife, your husband kill me. Your father kill me dead. Your husband kill you dead. Your father kill you dead. Cabba's dad kill me dead. Your brothers kill me dead. I take you for wife, we both get killed dead." I see she look sad so I speak more soft. "I want you for wife. I like your baby, but I don't want her for wife. But, I take you for wife, we all get killed dead. How can I take you for wife?"

She start cry. I put my hands on her shoulders, pull her head against my chest. She put her arms round me. When we close like that, that spell proper strong, I get that bang bang in my head and I feel stir between my legs. Then baby start cry too, and Jinggaya jump up. "I can't stay more," she say. "They hear Monanggu cry." And she pick up Monanggu and run off back to them other women.

Cabba's dad say soon we go again to lake in north. I think, how can I go to lake in north? How I leave Jinggaya, not see her for many seasons? I know I don't go to lake in north. I got to see Jinggaya.

Next time I see her, I say, "You want me for husband, we got to go away from this country. Got to go far away, leave no track, no one follow. Got to go in night, no one see. Got to go to new country, maybe other side of world, where old man prop up sky. Got to leave our own people. I got to leave my brothers and sisters and my fathers and mothers. You got to leave your brothers and sisters and fathers and mothers. You got to leave your husband too. Hard only two people and baby get water and tucker in strange country. Other mobs in strange country, maybe they kill us and eat us. Maybe no water or tucker for us in strange country. Maybe Cabba's dad point bone at us, kill us dead."

Jinggaya quiet. After a bit she say, "Clever man in my mob point bone too."

I don't say anything. I don't want leave my family. I don't want leave Borrudum and Cabba. I don't want hard life in strange country. But I don't want leave Jinggaya. I look at her face. She look at ground. I see she think. She think same as me. She cry. She cry proper quiet. She rock back and forward, cry proper quiet.

I put my hand on her shoulder. She put her arms round me, hug me. She put her head on my chest.

After a bit she stop crying. I kneel on ground, she sit across my lap proper close. My head go bang bang. She pull closer. We hug each other. She breathe hard. I breathe hard. We kiss kiss, fight for air for breathe. Soon we fly like pelican soar on top of sky. We leap like fish jump up silver flash from lake. Eyes shut we see colours like crimson rosella. We together, some magic make us one person.

After, Jinggaya say, "We got to make life together."

"You sure?" I say. "You know him hard life?" She sign yes. "We got to go proper quick, before my mob go to lake in north." She sign yes again. "Soon, Moon Man torch be full. We go at night, by light of Moon Man torch, walk plenty before anyone find we go. You let Sun Woman finish journey today, then journey over tomorrow, then when Moon-Man come over trees we meet here. Bring dilly with plenty tucker."

As she go, I say, "Don't tell anybody."

Then I call her again. "Jinggaya, Jinggaya! What your night name?"

She turn and smile. "Malilba. What yours?"

"Gunmyimbook." She laugh and run off.

At camp I ask Mother Berangu give me big dilly bag. I save dry meat, some shoot and yam and damper in this dilly. Also save mussel shells for scrape and carve, sharp stone for skin and cut meat, stones for spear point and stone for axe head, string and sinew for tie up, resin from grass tree, hard

47

stick for make fire, some paint. I look Cabba and Borrudum, want tell where I go, but can't. Then I think, what they think when I go? What my own mother and own father think? What Mother Berangu think? I go and no one know why, they think I fall off cliff or get bit by snake. They think I lie dead or dying, they search all over, don't find, don't know if I alive or dead. They think I dead, they mourn for me, they all sad for no reason.

Then last evening I go squat with Mother Berangu at her fire. I say, "Mother, you know I always good son to you."

She look at me long time, then say, "You best son any mother have, Bradek."

I quiet long time after that. Then I say, "Mother, what you think if I …" But I stop. I can't say that. I think, I tell Jinggaya don't tell anyone. How I tell Berangu?

"Yes, son?" I see by her eyes she know I in trouble. She want help me.

"What if I go away for a bit?"

"Away? Away, where? What you mean?" I silent. "You mean, away from our camp? You do that now when go hunt. Or, you mean, away from our mob?" I still silent. "Oh, no - away from our mob, from our country, that bad day for me, bad day for all your family here what love you. Why you think go away?"

I can't say anything. I can't look at Berangu. I look

in fire, feel wet come to eyes. I feel throat tight, feel like can't breathe good. Can't help this.

I feel Berangu hand on my shoulder. She put her head near mine, speak quiet in my ear. "You got woman, is that your trouble?" I don't say anything. Can't speak. I sense she nod her head. "Yes, that him, too right. You got woman draw you away. Well, I tell you, son, you not first man run off with woman. But you better be proper careful, for your dad kill you, and Cabba's dad kill you dead. You know that. You don't come back if you run off with woman. Your dad already fix you up with a wife."

Words of Berangu go in my body like spear. I in agony. Jinggaya, help me be strong! Goanna, help me now!

Hand of Berangu stroke my shoulder a bit. Then she say, still quiet, "Your mother Berangu always love you, whatever you do." I look at her face. Her eyes smile, I feel her love reach me. I hold her and put my cheek against her neck.

"I always love you, mother," I say.

*

Night come. I wait at place meet Jinggaya. That Moon Man, he high over trees but no sign of my woman. No cloud in sky. Moon Man light up whole plain, see long way. See smoke rise in sky from Mairkaioo fires to south. Dark under trees, don't see so much. I squat still under big gum. Small creature run between bushes, maybe possum. I see bat in sky, hear bats quarrel in tree nearby.

49

Insects click in trees, moth brush against my face. I hold waddy tight, for them *mamu* come about at night. Night air cold, I get cold from squat still with no fire, but don't want make noise. I got small possum skin rug, I put over shoulders keep warm. I got three short hunting spears and spear-thrower. I got long fishing spear which got four points. I got wide spear shield and narrow club shield. I got axe and throwing stick in waist string. I got my dilly full of them things. I think, where my woman?

Moon Man walk high in sky. I think, Jinggaya don't come. She get wrong night. She can't escape camp. She injured, fall down cliff, get bit by snake. She change mind, don't want leave her family. She don't love me, don't mean come away with me. She leave me here face *mamu* alone. I stupid. What Mother Berangu think when I go back in morning? She know I stupid. I think, maybe better I fall down cliff.

Then I hear noise, proper faint. Noise of footstep on leaf. I keep quiet, keep close to tree in dark. No noise then, but I know someone near. That someone keep proper quiet. Everything quiet, even bats. I listen good. I take good grip on waddy.

Then soft voice come, "Gunmyimbook?"

That voice proper quiet, but like a shout inside my head. I forget all problem and call back quiet, "Malilba?"

She soon come to me. She put Monanggu on ground. Monanngu sleep. We hug. I say, "Why you

50

don't come before this?"

She say, 'I can't leave our camp. They have corroboree, don't sleep, I scared they see me. Then Monanggu awake, not quiet. Then Moon Man too
high, they see me on grass so got to come by trees."
She shiver and say, 'Oh, this place so dark. *Mamu*
here, I sure."

"Them *mamu* don't know who we really are, we
safe if we use night name," I tell her. "We got to go
quick, now." I tie grass round her feet same like
mine. Then I ask her shut her eyes. When they shut,
I cut vein near my elbow, drop blood over her grass
and mine. That vein trick proper secret. That blood
proper good magic, make grass work better. When
I finish I say, 'Open eyes now. We got to leave no
tracks. If grass slip, tell me, I do again. Now, come
quick."

She pick up Monanggu and all her things. She got
big dilly full of stuff, possum skin rug, coolamon
with water in and digging stick. She say, 'Here,
drink water. Easier carry inside than in coolamon."
We both drink water, then I lead way quick to east.

When Moon Man go, we stop for a bit, wait for Sun
Woman. We walk in dark, we break plant, get
scratch, leave bits of blood or skin, make track easy
follow. So wait for light. We don't talk much. I
think about all I leave behind. I think Jinggaya
think same. We both quiet, but at first sign of
Sun-Woman we drink dew from leaves, fix grass on
feet again and walk proper quick to east.

Jinggaya know this east side of Mairkaioo country. I don't. We come to low hills, covered in bush. Jinggaya say she know a mob south of these hills. We can't meet this mob, they tell Mairkaioo where we go. We got to go straight up hills. We follow dry stream bed into thick bush. Sun Woman high in sky but we got plenty shade. We eat tucker from dilly. We got no water. I don't want cut plant or tree root for water, leave track easy follow. From hills we see over plain to south. We see fires of hunters in plain. Might be Mairkaioo, might be other mob. We keep behind trees, make no fire, go careful.

When Sun Woman go, we sleep, for too dark walk under trees. We don't make shelter but find fallen tree with roots like small cave, sleep there. In morning we drink dew, walk again. Three times Sun Woman rise up, we walk, then Sun Woman sleep, we sleep. We walk out of hills into strange country. Jinggaya don't know this country. I don't know this country. Mairkaioo don't come to this country. My mob don't come to this country. We free now. Now we got to make new life. We think, what sort of mob live in this country?

We come down hills from head of valley. We find stream, got good water, but we hungry. We follow stream down toward new open country. Jinggaya see possum nest in tree, want dig out. I say to Jinggaya, "We cut out that possum, them axe blows heard all over this bush, bring any stranger quick." Jinggaya say she want fire. I say to

Jinggaya, "We light fire now, our mob don't see, but maybe strange mob see. We got to look about first."

We go to where trees thin out at bottom of hill. We see smoke far off. I say to Jinggaya, "We light fire, that mob see our smoke proper quick. We got to find berry or root eat without cook."

Jinggaya don't say much but I see her look at ground proper careful. Then she dig with her stick. She dig up big yam. Only two tiny leaves come up on the ground, but she see them proper good. She see yam good, that woman. She say, "This yam cheeky, got to soak him good before eat or he make us crook." So we cut up yam and soak him till he not cheeky, then we eat him and he taste good.

Stream more wide soon and we got to wade across. I say to Jinggaya, "This good place make camp. Can't see smoke of strange mob."

Jinggaya laugh and say, "We make camp near water, I get baby!" That true, I think, water near woman often make baby. Them spirits live near water, they go into woman through belly button, make baby inside with help of man juice. But I tell her no worry, too soon since Monanggu born for more baby.

Plenty loose branch lie about, so we make wurly. Jinggaya go off get more yam or shoot, I go down stream hunt kangaroo. I see wallaby on short grass near stream. He eat grass, then look all around. His ears go up and turn all round, then he eat grass again. He keep good look out that wallaby. But he hungry, he eat quick. I put down spears and spear thrower, for can't kill wallaby with spear. Can only kill wallaby with club. I pick up branch with leaves, hold out in front for cover, creep close proper slow. I got waddy in other hand. Each time that wallaby pick up his head for look about, I stop, don't move. Then when he eat, I creep. When I creep, game I play when young come in my head. I see all them young men belong our mob in line They hold their waddies ready. Two men a short way off, they got a green twig bent into a ring. Granddad Loolunar come, say to young men, "This ring wallaby". Them two men throw that ring one to other and all us young men see wallaby jump. We throw our waddies at him as he pass. First young man to hit wallaby get called best hunter, he stand out and others go on. Last young man left get called worst hunter. First time I play this game, I last. I get shame. Them young men say, "You never get wallaby, you worst hunter in world!" I get shame every time I remember this.

Take long time get close to that wallaby. I so close I hear crunch as he bite on grass and chew. He see me, start hop off. He jump off fast. I stand up quick, follow his run. Then I throw waddy. That waddy fly through air, spin all time. He get wallaby full in body. That wallaby fall to ground. I run and finish him with hit on head. This proper good wallaby, I proud take him to Jinggaya!

I carry wallaby back on shoulders. Jinggaya already back from get woman tucker, she go wild when see wallaby. She say, "Bradek, you proper good hunter!" That time most happy time.

Sun Woman low in sky. No sign of strange mob, so I make fire while Jinggaya give breast to Monanggu. Find dry soft wood start fire. My fire drill, he proper hard stick. I drill him into soft wood, on and on. Drill him plenty. That soft wood break up into dust. Drill more, that wood begin to smoke. Blow on dust, him make small flame. I feed small flame with bark strip, make big flame. Then build fire with good dry wood so not much smoke. We soon got big hot fire. I let him die down a bit, then scrape hole with waddy, bury that wallaby in hot ashes. He soon cook, we pull him out and eat all we can.

When we finish, night time come. We got big bellies, hard move about. We build up fire for light, sit together by fire. I hold Jinggaya round waist. We both look at fire. I see light of fire wave on Jinggaya face. She look happy. She look beautiful. Baby asleep in wurly behind us. Jinggaya turn to me, put hand on my shoulder, stroke my cheek with other hand. She say, "I never so happy, Gunmyimbook."

I tell her I never so happy too. "You happy when you child?" I ask.

She go quiet. I see she think. Then she say, slow, "Yes, I happy when I child. I play in water a lot with other children. We run, swim, laugh a lot. I very happy when I child. I got good friends, good sisters. But all that change when I woman."

I got question, but first time I talk like this to

woman, so don't know how ask. She see I want ask question. She give me smile. I say, "How you become woman?"

"How you mean?" she say.

I not sure what I mean. "You know," I say, "like Thurumulan make me a man."

"Oh," she say, "like that?" She point at my cock where hood cut off.

"Yes."

She laugh a little. "True Thurumulan come and cut off skin? Not done by men of your mob?"

"You know I can't tell you secret of that ceremony. Thurumulan come, he take skin and tooth. That all I can tell."

"Oh," she say. She sound like she hope I say more. "Well, no magic make me woman. Old woman of our mob take me when I start bleed, cut me inside with sharp stone, make room for cock and baby. After that, I woman. I already live in camp belong husband. When I woman, he start sex with me ..."

She stop quick, look sad. I think she not happy when husband start sex with her. I see water in her eyes pick up light of fire. I stroke her arm. Then she cry a bit and say, "Oh, Gunmyimbook, I don't like be made woman. That not good time."

"But you made into beautiful woman. You got to be happy be beautiful. All women like be beautiful."

"Oh, Gunmyimbook, you don't know! I wish I made ugly!"

I sit up more. I don't understand. I say, "Oh no! Why you want be made ugly? I like you beautiful."

She stop cry and stroke my chest. "You good man, Bradek. I know first time I see you, you good man. I like be beautiful for you."

"That true? First time? I same, I like you first time I see. Why you run away when I come see you next time?"

"Oh, I scared …. I don't expect magic work so good."

I sit right up. I don't understand. "How you mean, magic?"

She look like not sure speak or not speak. Then she smile and stroke my chest again. "You don't know? Don't you feel that magic pull you to me?"

I think, how she know this what I feel? "Yes, I feel that magic. That magic keep me awake at night, make me think of you, make me go find you in millet country. How you know about that magic?"

She laugh. Only small laugh. I love that small laugh she got. Each time she make that small laugh, that small laugh make me happy. She see I smile at her. She say, "True you don't know, do you?" She laugh again. I laugh too. Can't help that when she laugh. "Well, now I tell you truth. I get love spell put on you!"

This news hit me like rock. "How you mean, love spell?" But I know what she mean, I hear of same spell in our mob but never try him myself.

"Why, you know … I got aunt, she good friend, she always want help me, she know all them spells. I tell her I want you for lover. She say I got to have something belong you. Only thing I got is your footprint. I take her, show her your footprint. I already put my footprint inside. When she see this, she say I do right thing. Then she sing proper good love spell over footprints. She know all them spell. All those women in our mob want her spells. Well, she sing that spell proper good, don't she?"

We both laugh and I got to agree she sing that spell proper good. Then I say, "But I don't get no love spell put on you."

Jinggaya say, "You don't need to!" and laugh more. We proper happy.

What she say before still trouble me. "If you want me for lover, why you want be ugly? I like you beautiful."

She look sad again. She quiet long time. Then she say, "You got *ch---* ceremony in your mob?" I don't remember now exact name she call that ceremony.

"*Ch---*? I don't know that. What *ch---*?"

"He secret ceremony. Only old men do him. They have big secret ceremony, big dance, sing, lots of magic. I don't know what they do. At end they all a bit mad. They choose a few women got to go to ceremony at end. Maybe choose five women and one more. They all put their cocks inside all them women. All them men and all them women. Them women got to do this. They choose beautiful women. They choose me all the time. Some women, they say they like, but I don't like. I don't like at all, I hate. I don't like, him make me feel proper crook."

I feel my throat swallow but can't say anything. We don't have ceremony like that in our mob. Or, if we do, I don't know him.

Jinggaya quiet again. Then she say, "I fix them last time they do that ceremony. I put sand all up between my legs. I fill up with sand, they can't get their cocks in, him all rough. They don't like. They angry, they beat me, but I don't care."

She quiet for a bit again. Then, "That why ugly better."

I angry they treat Jinggaya bad. I tell her I angry, I tell her I happy she come away with me, I tell her I don't give her to other men.

She say, "I happy I beautiful for you. You good to me. I good wife for you, you see. But them men in our mob, they don't like me now, I afraid they get clever man point bone."

"He can't point bone if he don't know which way we go. We hide tracks proper good, they never know."

Jinggaya give me small kiss kiss. "I hope we always happy like this," she say.

"I hope we always happy like this, too. I think, Goanna help us get away. He look after us now too. You paint Goanna sign on my body now? Good I show I Goanna, make sure he look after us."

Jinggaya say she paint Goanna sign if I show her how. I get paint from dilly, grind up and mix with blood from secret vein while she don't look. Then I show her how paint sign all over my chest. When done, I feel good and say to Jinggaya, "Malilba, this proper good sign you paint. Now Goanna look after us and keep us safe."

Whell I wake next morning, before Sun Woman come, I feel something wrong. I wake up Jinggaya, tell her keep Monanggu quiet.

"What happen?" she say.

"I don't know," I say. "Something wrong. Stay in wurly, I look."

I crawl out of wurly. Light of Sun Woman come faint at edge of sky. I look about, see nothing. My spears still stick in ground where I put them night before. I stand near spears. I put throwing stick in waist string, at back where no one see. I pick up shield and waddy.

"What happen?" call Jinggaya from wurly. She got Monanggu to breast.

"I don't know," I say. "I think strangers come near.

60

Maybe they see we eat their wallaby, they angry."

I wait and keep look out. We on grassy bit near river. Up stream, where we come from, I see plenty trees. Down stream, grass open out more into plain where we see stranger smoke before. I stare into trees, see nothing. I stare into plain. In dim light I see one feller stand. He don't move. He stand still long way off, look my way. He stand on one leg, got foot of other leg on knee. He lean on spear thrower.

Light get brighter. When I sure he see me, I put down shield and waddy, hold up hand with fist for torch, show I friend. That feller, he start walk my way, proper slow. He walk, he stop. He walk again, then stop again. He hold up his fist. He got spear thrower in hand but he got no spear. He got waist string. I think, he got throwing stick in back, same like me. He walk again. I think, he walk proper slow. He don't walk normal. Then I think, he walk like man carry spear in toes. That old trick, pick up spear between toes, keep hid slide through grass. We all do this as children, do over and over until proper good, can pick up spear in thrower and throw all proper quick. I keep near my spears and shield in case need. That feller come closer then stop again. He about a spear throw away.

He not like any other feller I see. He tall feller, with big beard and hair tied up on top of head. He got bone through nose. White bone stick out both sides of nose. He got string round neck with feathers on him. He got long scars make pattern across chest, like scars from burn not scars from cut. I see him look at me, look at my feet, look at my spears. I see him look at our fire. He see what left of our wallaby near fire. He see back of our wurly, maybe guess woman inside. I say quiet to Jinggaya, "I see stranger here. Stay in wurly." I see she look scared. Don't blame her, I scared. That bone scary.

Stranger circle finger round his face then point to his bone. I think, he ask me why I got no bone. Maybe all his mob got bones. I don't know how answer. I point back way we come, show him way we come, point that way then point at feet where we now. I show fist again, show friend.

He make fist with two fingers up, twist them fingers like wallaby ears. He point our wallaby, then tap own chest. He say, that wallaby my wallaby. I point belly, make pull waist belt tight, show we hungry.

He put out hand flat, wave like water. He point at stream, then tap own chest. He say, that water my water. I open mouth, point tongue and throat, show we thirsty.

He keep look at me. I look back. Still he look at me long time, sign nothing. I think, why he look at me long time? He don't try look in wurly. He don't walk about. He look at me. I look back at him. I think, he try get me look back at him. Then I look over my shoulder quick. I see two young feller creep up behind. They got spears in their throwers. They got bones in their noses. They got hair tied up. They come kill me.

I grab my shield and a spear quick and jump around. I angry and scared same time. I give roar. I shout "You keep away!" They stop creep, step back surprised. I turn look at old man. He don't move much, I can spear him before he spear me. I look one way then the other, shout, "Keep away!" again. They don't seem sure what do. Then Jinggaya come run out of wurly. She run up near me, pick up digging stick. She stand behind me and shake digging stick at men. "Keep away!" she shout. She strong woman, she look fierce. I glad have her on my side.

Them men surprised, don't know what do. Jinggaya and me, we circle. They crouch, they wait. I think, no one want start real fight. Jinggaya and me circle more, show we ready for fight. Then out of trees come another feller of their mob. He got bone in nose. He got hair tied up. He carry spear but not in thrower. Other fellers look at him like he tell them what do. He stand there, don't make threat. He look at me. Then he call out, 'Stop!' He say this word funny but I know him 'stop'. He say this to other feller of his mob and I see they stop make threat. Then this new feller walk down from trees toward me.

He carry spear upright and hold up hand with fist. I stand my spear upright and Jinggaya let digging stick hang, show we ready talk. This feller keep walk, careful, keep watch. I take quick look over shoulder. Other fellers don't move. I let new feller come closer. He not old like first feller, not young like other fellers. His face don't show anger. I show him my face got no anger, and he come more close.

63

He got mark of spear on shoulder. He got mark of spear on thigh. Thumb of his fist all crushed. He fight plenty. He got string round neck, hang something under arm, don't see what. He look my face. I look his face. He got good face, strong face, face like clever man, face like good warrior. I think, I like man got that face for friend, not for enemy. Then he stop quite close, and point to my chest.

'Goanna,' he say. He say this funny, but I know what he mean. He lift one leg, put hand to foot, then lift other leg, put other hand to foot. This like walk of goanna.

I look back at him. 'Me Goanna,' I say and bang hand on chest. I do goanna walk.

He look pleased. Then he call to old feller, 'This man Goanna!' He put his hand on his own chest and he say to me, 'Me Goanna!' Then he point to old feller and say, 'That old feller Goanna!' He stick spear in ground and let go. He call to two young feller, 'This man Goanna! He my brother!'

I think, maybe this trick but then see old feller pick spear out of toes and plant in ground. Then he walk up with no weapon and show fist. When he close, he touch his chest and say, 'Me Goanna!' He smile. 'We friend.'

They touch my arms. I let them. They take good look at Jinggaya. 'This your woman?' ask old feller.

'She my wife,' I say. 'She Black Cockatoo.'

Old feller say, "You young have wife like that. You don't even get a bone yet." All this he say in funny way, but I know what he mean.

I say, "We don't wear bones in our mob. I man. I got my cock slit." I show him my slit and I see he surprised.

"That like kangaroo cock," he say. I see he know power of my slit. "You got good magic." Then he say, "We got more Goanna in our mob. You come with us, you meet your brothers."

While Jinggaya get Monanggu and dilly, I ask them strangers if they want eat what left of wallaby. They say yes, and they all eat a bit of that wallaby. In wurly, I find Jinggaya look troubled. I ask her what trouble her. She say, she don't want sex with Nose-Bones. She say, her old husband always make her have sex with strangers, make peace. I tell her I don't share her with any other man. She happy hear this. Then we all walk downstream, to the plain where we see smoke day before. That party of Nose-Bones, they hide kangaroo and emu they get before, pick them up and take them back to their camp. They already cook that kangaroo and emu before hide, so don't stink when get back to camp.

On way, old feller Goanna tell me his name Ilkari. Other feller Goanna tell me his name Daingumbo. Daingumbo say his own brother killed dead when he small. He say I his own brother come back.

Sun Woman travel over sky three times before we come near Nose-Bone camp. We wade through plenty swamp, plenty water. I learn Nose-Bone don't move about much like my mob. They tell me they got water in river all time, fish in river all time, only move small way up or down river get near woman tucker when fruit or berry or shoot in season. They say men go long way hunt kangaroo.

Jinggaya and me, we scared go in Nose-Bone camp, but all women and children come out meet us. Clever men of their mob come meet us, ask questions, then go. Daingumbo take us to his wurly. This not like wurly of my mob. He big, we can nearly stand. He got flat sides slope down from ridge. Daingumbo got wife and children. We meet wife and children belong Daingumbo. Wife belong Daingumbo got two skulls hang from belt. Jinggaya stay with wife belong Daingumbo while Daingumbo take me meet other Goannas. They glad see me, but first thing they say is, "Why you got no nose-bone? You not man?"

They take me Goanna place and we do Goanna dance. We know we brothers. After, I paint Goanna sign on rock. They all pleased, tell me I paint Goanna sign proper good. Old man Ilkari squat by sign and sing Goanna song. That song, him all in old language. I don't understand all them words, but I know that song tell story how Goanna come from Dreamtime. That song proper beautiful song. We don't have song like that in my mob. I tell them about Goanna Rock. They say Goanna Rock proper sacred place, they never see him.

When I see Jinggaya next I say, 'Goanna look after us proper good, keep us safe."

She say, "That Goanna, he powerful spirit. I glad he look after us."

I say, "These Nose-Bones good fellers. We stay here."

She say, "I like wife belong Daingumbo. I glad we stay here."

I say, "I got to get bone through nose, like other men this mob."

She say nothing for a bit. Then, "You got to get bone through nose, I know."

I say, "I got to go to Goanna Rock, make ceremony, thank Goanna for look after us."

Jinggaya say nothing.

I stay Nose-Bone camp while Moon Man torch get thin. Them Nose-Bones happy when I say I got to get bone through nose. We have big dance, big feast. I scared about hole through nose, but Daingumbo say he don't hurt. We men go off, they make platform same like my initiation. Daingumbo pinch with his fingers between my nostrils, their clever man make hole with sharp bone point. I pretend he don't hurt, like Daingumbo say, but he do. Then they put in short white bone from wattle bird leg. They give me new name, Nantoomana, which in their lingo mean 'Kangaroo-Cock'. After, come back, all women and children join in dance. Jinggaya look at me long time, then start laugh. I laugh too. We have proper good time. Daingumbo give me his wife. I think he want me give him Jinggaya. I feel bad not take wife belong Daingumbo, but I tell him his wife belong him and Jinggaya belong me. I tell him feller in my mob don't lend his wife to stranger. This not true, but I hear of mob where true. I think Daingumbo hear of this mob too, for he don't argue.

Jinggaya ask, "What Daingumbo got hang under his arm?" I tell her I don't know. I don't like tell her he look like hand cut off man.

When Moon Man torch get big again, I tell Jinggaya I got to go make ceremony at Goanna Rock. She say she don't want me go away, but I tell her I come back soon. I take big dilly full of tucker and paint. I leave when Sun Woman get up next morning.

I go back way we come. When go back other side of hills, I tie grass on feet again so don't get tracked. Don't see no one. That side of hills proper dry, creeks empty, my mob and them Mairkaioo gone where more water and tucker. After a bit, come to old camp belong my mob. This camp like I don't know him, wurlies fall down, no feller about, no smoke from fire place, no noise from children, no dogs. Only noise from my feet tread on dry gum leaves, buzz of cicadas in the trees and call from some birds who don't yet go to new water. I push through bush up to Goanna Rock. I get Goanna board, put him on rock, do Goanna dance thank Goanna for keep me and Jinggaya safe. Then I paint over Goanna sign on rock, make him clear and bright colour. Some of that colour I mix with blood from secret vein so good magic. When all done I hide board and go back to empty camp.

That camp strange. I go to wurly belong my dad. I think, here where my dad plant his spears, there where my mum grind seed, there where Berangu weave dilly. I see ash of their fire. I see where plant now grow over fire place. They go many days, while Moon Man torch get thin then grow fat again. I go to young man camp. I think, here where Cabba mend spear, there where Borrudum carve spear thrower. I go to wurly belong Cabba's dad. I think, here where Cabba's dad think his *yowi* out of that *mulowil*, come visit my *yowi*.

On trail north side of camp I find baby. That baby proper dead, him eaten by ants and birds. I think, I know mother of that baby. That mother, she full with baby before I leave camp. I think, that baby born soon after I leave camp. That mother, she already got one small baby. That mother can't carry two baby when mob go north. I think, that mother can't carry new baby when mob go north. She ask other woman carry other baby, but no woman got spare hand. I think, she don't want leave new baby behind but clever men of our mob tell her she got to kill that baby. She can't bear kill baby, so she just leave him behind. I think, when she come back find baby dead, she so bad troubled she cut off one of her fingers for mourn baby.

I bury baby, put stick in ground mark place.

I go down creek look for water. That creek, he all dry but I see green leaf about. I think, that creek got

69

water below ground, got to dig him up. I go up creek, look for good place dig. I see good place, where trees near creek, make shade. Then I see hole already made in that place. No water in hole. That hole made some days before I come. Our mob always leave before got to dig for water. When got to dig for water, not enough water for whole mob. That hole, he made after mob leave for lake in north. I think, who come here after mob leave for lake in north?

I go to hole proper careful. I see where hands scrape earth out of hole. I see track of feller make hole. That feller injured. I see mark of hand belong that feller on ground, see mark where he pull his body along ground, see where one foot push, where other foot slide. That feller got one leg injured. He crawl to creek, he dig for water, he pull himself away into shade. If he still alive, maybe he lie in trees near creek.

In creek bed I see one good foot print. Toes gather, foot print of woman. Sole flat, foot print of old woman. I think, I know that foot print. That look like foot print belong Mother Berangu.

I follow trail from creek bed. He take me into bush beside creek. I look into bush. Under leaves and branches I see Mother Berangu. I think she dead.

I crawl in beside her. She still a bit warm. I put her head in my arm. She stir a bit. I see her arm twitch. That arm proper thin, like she don't eat long time. I see her leg all swollen. Her eyes stay shut. Her lips part, but she don't speak. I see them lips all

70

cracked, like she don't drink long time. She got big coolamon beside her. I put her down, take coolamon, run to creek bed, dig out more hole with waddy. After a bit small pool of water seep in hole. Not much water in that creek. I get little bit water in coolamon, carry to Mother Berangu, drop in lips. Only few drops. That not enough. I go back to creek, see mallee tree. I dig down deep round tree root. While I dig, I remember Mother Berangu tell me about mallee tree when I small. She say in Dreamtime there are two brothers, one he take care, he carry coolamon full of water when he go hunt, other don't care, he don't take water. When they in dry place, they thirsty, and careful brother don't share water. He say other brother got to carry own water. Other brother grab for coolamon and spill water all over ground. That water spill everywhere, he fill up the creeks and flood all the land. Both them brothers drown in that flood. The water still rise, and the birds get troubled and say they got to build a dam stop that flood. Them birds pick up roots of the mallee tree and build a dam stop the flood. That why roots of mallee tree always full of water.

I find root, long like long spear, thick like my arm. I cut him with axe. That root got plenty water. I run back to Mother Berangu, hold tree root over mouth. That root drip drip steady into mouth. She cough a bit, but I see she swallow water. She cough more, then her eyes open a bit. She look at me, then she look scared and shut eyes again. Then I remember I got bone in nose. I take out bone, and say to her, "Mother Berangu, this is Bradek hold you, give you

71

water."

She open her eyes again. This time I see she know me. She try say something. I think she try say my name, but no word come. She too dry, too weak. I go get more water, give her drink, then go away look for tucker. I eat all in my dilly. No tucker in that place. I hungry too. I look on bush for berry, but no berry. I look along creek for shoot, but no shoot. Them women our mob pick all berry and dig up all shoot. I look for possum and bandicoot, but them women catch all them possum and bandicoot. I peel bark off tree, find grubs, take back to Mother Berangu. She eat grubs. I go look more. In clear patch I find fresh dug earth. This where women of our mob dig yam. Them women always leave baby yam, grow into big yam when they get back. I dig up baby yam, take to Mother Berangu. She eat baby yam. I eat baby yam too.

Need more tucker. I go hunt through bush, don't find much. Then I see big goanna on tree. He crawl up trunk of tree. He rest through this season. He big goanna. His body length of my arm, his tail length of my leg. I think, I don't eat goanna. I don't eat my brother. Then I think, Berangu eat goanna. That goanna, he sent by Goanna spirit for Berangu. I sing thank you to Goanna spirit and get that goanna with my waddy. I walk up to tree easy. He don't move a bit. He know why he sent there.

I make fire and cook that goanna good. I give goanna to Mother Berangu. She eat like proper hungry woman. I look at that goanna. I think, Bradek don't eat own brother. Then I look at Berangu eat goanna. I think, maybe Goanna spirit mean for Bradek eat goanna this time. So I eat goanna too. He good tucker for proper hungry man.

By and by Mother Berangu speak. She say she stupid. She have sex with man of our mob. My dad don't say she can, that man not brother of my dad. He find them. He hit her with waddy on leg. She say that leg break, she can't walk. She say my dad spear that man in thigh. She say our mob can't stay this camp, got no water and got no tucker. Got to go to lake in north. She say they got to leave her. They put her in trees with coolamon of water and some tucker. She drink all that water and eat all that tucker. She crawl to creek, dig hole for water, get some, crawl back to trees when Sun Woman high in sky. There she think she don't go back for more water, she too weak. Maybe time she join Dreamtime spirits. She not sure if she with Dreamtime spirits. She ask, "You spirit of Bradek?"

I tell her I not spirit.

She say, "I think I see bone through your nose."

I say, "Mother, you see bone through my nose. I that Bradek who run off with Jinggaya. She Black Cockatoo from Mairkaioo mob. We run off far, come live with Nose-Bone mob other side of world. Now my name Kangaroo-Cock."

She say, "You look like my son. Bradek."

"I am your son. Bradek."

'I know you. You run off with Jinggaya. We hear this from Mairkaioo. Jinggaya tell her sister before she go. Sister say aunt belong Jinggaya put love-spell on you."

I angry Jinggaya tell sister. I tell her don't tell anyone. I say to Berangu, "True I run off with Jinggaya. True her aunt put love-spell on me. I happy get love-spell. I happy get Jinggaya. She beautiful woman and she got happy nature, too. She laugh a lot. She make me laugh. I tell her don't tell anyone we run off."

Mother Berangu look troubled. 'She tell her sister. When Jinggaya go, her father get mad. Her husband get mad. They make that sister tell them the truth. She say you run away to east. Father and husband and brother belong Jinggaya, they make big war party, they search all over east. They don't find your tracks. They say they kill you with spear in thigh, kill Jinggaya dead. They don't find you. They come back, meet with your dad and Cabba's dad. Your dad say he kill you dead. Cabba's dad say he kill you dead. They go out look for you, don't find you. You got to make sure you don't see your dad or Cabba's dad, they kill you dead. They mad angry."

Berangu go quiet and close her eyes like she tired. I say quiet, 'Don't you be troubled, Mother. Jinggaya and me, we on other side of world. We safe, we don't come back."

She wake up, look troubled again. 'No, no, Bradek," she say. 'I got to tell you – that husband

74

belong Jinggaya, he get clever man of Mairkaioo point bone at Jinggaya. That clever man, he point bone to east, he sing Jinggaya dead. I tell you, he sing your woman. Your woman dead."

Berangu sleep. I fill coolamon with water, leave goanna beside her and run off quick back to Nose-Bone country. I run quick, sleep only when Moon Man put out his torch. Only when I wake I think, you stupid, Bradek. You most stupid man on this earth. You run off so quick you forget tie grass on feet. Now you got to hope your track too old for your own dad and Cabba's dad follow when they get back from lake in north.

No time think about that, got to get to Jinggaya proper quick.

When I get near Nose-Bone camp I think, my Jinggaya already dead. But no, she come out meet me. Them Nose-Bone women gather tucker all about, keep look out for me, send smoke say I come back. Then Jinggaya run out meet me.

"I happy see you," she say.

"I happy see you still alive," I say. "I find Mother Berangu, she proper crook with broken leg. She say clever man of your mob point bone at you!"

Jinggaya stare at me. I see her mouth open, but no word come. Her eyes open wide, they bulge out. I never see anyone look like that before. Her ears

75

stick out, her hair stick out. Her eyes turn inside out so all white, and she fall to ground. "Jinggaya!" I call, "don't die!" But I think she already dead. Her arms all limp, she don't move.

I don't know what do. I look about. I see some women over camp way, but they can't help. No men I can see. I pick up Jinggaya body, look all about. No one. Then I think, only one person can help. That person Goanna. I pull Jinggaya against Goanna sign on my chest and I sing to Goanna, "Goanna! You best brother I ever have! You look after me from Dreamtime! Now, help me save Jinggaya!"

I stay there with Jinggaya body. She don't move. By and by, I see man run out of bush into plain. He run toward me. He carry spear and shield. He Nose-Bone. He Daingumbo, my brother. He run up, plant spear and pant. "What happen?" he ask.

I don't understand. "How you know I need you?" I ask.

"I hear your voice call. The hand of my father tell me where find you. I tell you more later – but what happen to your woman?"

"Clever man of her mob point bone and sing her dead!"

He grab Jinggaya from me and put his ear to her chest. He say, "She not dead yet! But she die. We got to take her to our camp."

We carry Jinggaya to camp. Soon everyone know

Jinggaya die from point of bone. They all come round Daingumbo wurly, many people. They all point and speak quiet. I hear them say, "Bone point that Black Cockatoo woman. She proper dead damn quick."

Daingumbo stand before them. He beat his chest. He say, "No one got magic stronger than Nose-Bone magic! We got to save Nantoomana woman! Ask Grandfather Parangal help save Nantoomana woman."

I go with Daingumbo and that crowd to south side of camp. We all gather round wurly belong Grandfather Parangal. Daingumbo call out, "Grandfather Parangal, my brother Goanna, Nantoomana, need your help! You got to help save his woman from point of bone!"

Some sound come from inside this wurly. I don't know what sound. Like grunt. Then Daingumbo go inside. He gone short time, then he come out. He hold up old feller. This old feller, he so old he can't walk good. I never see anybody so old before. Any feller so old in our mob, he get left behind, can't keep up. Old feller like that in Guringbadawah mob, they strangle him with grass cord, then all his children eat him up, remember him good. We don't eat our own feller in my old mob, we don't like kill dead our own feller, so we leave them behind. This old Nose-Bone feller, he so old Daingumbo got to hold him up.

This old feller name Parangal. He got bone through nose. He got no hair on top of head. He got beard thin and grey. He got pelican feet on string round neck. He carry old dilly. He limp up near me.

"You Nantoomana?" he ask. His voice like creak of old gum tree in night wind.

"I Nantoomana," I answer him.

"Show me your cock," he say. I show him. He say, "That proper good cock. That strong magic. You good warrior, never die in battle!"

I happy hear this. I see Nose-Bones step back when I come, I hear them whisper, "He got strong magic, that Nantoomana. Parangal say he never die in battle." Then Parangal wave his hand toward Daingumbo wurly and Daingumbo help him forward. Crowd step back more and I see that Parangal proper clever man, every feller there make way for him. Daingumbo say to me in quiet voice, "Grandfather Parangal most clever man in our mob after my own father."

We go towards wurly belong Daingumbo. Grandfather Parangal go slow, he fall behind. We go back. Parangal hold up his hand. We see some kind of light shine out of his hand. Then Parangal look at all them people go to that wurly. He got eyes that see right in a person. He say, "You go on, I see you there."

We all run to wurly belong Daingumbo. We get there panting. I look inside. Inside that wurly, we see Grandfather Parangal. He look at me with them strong eyes. I don't know how he get there first. All us young men run all way. I say, "Grandfather

Parangal, how you get here before us?"

He say, "I fly here on magic cord. I fly anywhere on magic cord. You see by and by. But now got to look at your woman quick." I think, I don't understand this. Maybe this some kind of trick. But how that old feller get there before all us young feller? Maybe he got that magic cord like he say. I don't have more time think about this, got to look after Jinggaya.

We look at Jinggaya. She lie there on possum skin rug. She don't move. Parangal touch her arm, then say, "This woman die."

I got to go out of wurly. I feel crook. I don't want Jinggaya die.

Parangal and Daingumbo come out. Parangal say to me, "Go to river. Get strip of reed from river. Get small branch of tea tree. Get feather of teal. Bring here quick."

I run to river. Plenty reed grow, I get strip. Plenty tea tree grow, I get small branch. Plenty teal on water, I go to their night place on bank, pick up feather there. I run back.

When I get back, I see Parangal finish draw stick in dirt outside wurly, make pattern. I don't know this pattern, he Nose-Bone magic pattern. Parangal take fire stick from Daingumbo fire, start small fire in pattern. On this fire he put reed strip. Reed strip too wet for burn, he curl up and go black with black smoke. Parangal say, "Black smoke good." He put tea tree branch on fire. Tea tree leaves crackle and burn with black smoke. Parangal say, "Black smoke good." He put teal feather on fire. Teal feather make black smoke. Parangal say, "Black smoke good."

Then he sit in front of pattern and fire. He sit with legs crossed. He hold his pelican feet and he sing. That song he sing, I don't know him. Them words old words, proper old words, I don't know them. He sing long time. He rock back and forward. He tell me he sing to spirit, he go visit spirit of Nose-Bones get help for Jinggaya. He close his eyes and sing more. In my own mind, I sing again to Goanna, ask him for help.

When song done, Parangal open eyes quick and say to me, "Come." I help him back into wurly. He kneel beside Jinggaya. I squat other side. He start sing again, very quiet. He reach in dilly bag, take out shell. That shell full of black paste. With his finger he take out paste and rub him over Jinggaya heart. She don't move. She got her eyes open, but I know she don't see me. Parangal still sing. Then, proper quick, he push his hand into paste and into Jinggaya body. When he pull his hand out, he covered in blood from Jinggaya heart. I look at his hand and I see he hold some bone. "Ah!" he say. "See, this the bone! He stick in Jinggaya heart! I take out!" He pass me that bone, with Jinggaya blood on him, and I see he short bone from leg of kangaroo, sharpened to point.

I say, "This short bone from leg of kangaroo! This that bone them clever men use for point! You proper clever man, you catch that bone, take him

80

out good!"

As I say this, Jinggaya let out sound like crow, "Ka-aa-aaaa." I put my arm under her neck, pull her up. She blink. I say, 'This clever man of Nose-Bones take out that bone your mob point! You safe!" I show her bone. She blink again, and I know she see me. I so happy. "You safe!" I say again. She smile back at me. When she smile like that, I know she safe. I never so happy in my life. I got water in eyes, I hug my Jinggaya. She don't die.

Parangal look like he got water in eye too. He say, "That right. She safe now. She don't die."

I say, "You proper clever man, this Nose-Bone magic proper powerful." He nod his head, then ask Daingumbo take him back.

I get water and food for Jinggaya. I feel in black paste. That hole he heal up proper good. No sign of that hole any more. That Nose-Bone magic proper powerful. Jinggaya soon sit up. She say, 'I feel good. I live." We kiss kiss.

"You miss me?" I ask.

'I miss you a lot," she say. I tell her all about Berangu. I don't tell her about forget grass on feet. I ask her what she do when I away. She say, 'I go with Daingumbo wife gather tucker. She tell me a lot about Nose-Bones. They not like our mobs."

"How you mean?"

"They always fight."

I laugh. "Huh, my mob always fight. Your mob always fight. Plenty fights in our mobs."

She say, "No, not fight like our mobs. Not fight one man against one man for steal wife like in our mobs. Not fight in open like our mobs. They got big fight with mob in next country. They go at night, kill in secret. Other mob come at night, kill in secret. Other mob, they called Googerak. Them Googerak take land down river belong Nose-Bones. Nose-Bones take back. Nose-Bones and Googerak fight all time, kill dead plenty. Nose-Bones eat the skin off them Googerak."

I don't say much. I think, this woman talk. But then Daingumbo come back. He happy see Jinggaya safe. He say to me, "Nantoomana, we happy Jinggaya don't die. We happy Grandfather Parangal say you don't die in battle. Now you come with us fight Googerak down river. Get your spear and shield. We go now!"

We go downstream while Sun Woman cross three times. We wade through plenty swamp. Us Nose-Bones number five and five more. Don't see Googerak. See their wurlies and tracks. They go off in bush to south.

Daingumbo say, "This land belong Nose-Bones. Them Googerak come here, take land. We fight them Googerak."

We make camp by river, spear fish for tucker. That

river got clay on his banks. We cover all body in clay, make body white like ghost, scare them Googerak. We dance by river after Sun Woman go, claim all that land for Nose-Bones.

We all rest when Daingumbo get up quick, look about.

"What happen?" I ask. He sign me finger on lips, keep quiet. Everybody stir, get shield and spear.

"Them Googerak about," say Daingumbo in proper quiet voice. "The hand of my father pinch me, wake me up, give warning."

"The hand of your father?" I ask.

He show me the hand he got on that string made from possum fur. String round neck, hand hang under left arm. "My father most clever man we ever know," he say. "Them Googerak kill him dead. That most sad day for all of our mob. We sew his body up in possum skin rugs. After three days, sacred oil from his body collect in them rugs. All the men and boys of our mob smear that oil on their own bodies, swear avenge death of my father. When all flesh leave his body, I cut off his right hand for keep remember him good. Now his hand pinch me when enemy near."

He take the hand of his father in his two hands and point him to east. "Which way they come?" he ask. "This way?" Then he point to south. "This way?" he ask again. Same with west and north. He say to me, "Hand of my father shake when I point him right way. But he don't shake now, I think he tired." He hold up hand again and shake him. 'Speak!" he say in angry voice. 'Speak, or I throw you to the dogs!'

Then he say, 'Look, hand of my father shake!" and I see that hand shaking. Them enemy, them Googerak, they come from south.

We get our other weapons, waddies and throwing sticks. Daingumbo say wade down river. That way Googerak don't hear us, we leave no tracks, don't lose way, for Moon Man torch small and behind cloud some time. That river bed stony, we got to walk careful, use spear thrower for walking stick. After we walk long time, we see light of fire on bank. Daingumbo say, 'That Googerak fire! Go quiet!' We go proper quiet and slow, like stalk kangaroo. We see three fires; maybe only three Googerak in that place. Daingumbo say in quiet voice, 'They sleep!'

We creep all round their camp. We creep proper slow, make no sound. I hear bang bang in ears but not made by think about Jinggaya. I think, if Jinggaya see me now, she proper scared. I proper scared too.

We see them by the light of their fires. They sleep. Only four of them. They all asleep, they don't know we there. They dream about hunt kangaroo, spear fish, have sex, maybe dream about kill Nose-Bones. They don't know we there. Then Daingumbo let out shout, and we all run in and kill them Googerak. I drive my spear right through a Googerak feller, pin him to ground. They all pinned to ground. Them Googerak wriggle and call out, but they can't move, they pinned. They pretty damn quick all killed dead. Daingumbo let out great roar, he shout, "Death of my father avenged!" and he wave his father's hand and kiss him. We all shout and dance, we proper fired up. When them Googerak fellers proper dead we pull them to fire. I see they got bones in their noses. I see they got their hair tied up. I don't expect this. I think, them Googerak like Nose-Bone mob. My old mob not like Nose-Bone mob. I think, strange two mobs almost same fight big war yet Nose-Bone mob take me as brother.

Daingumbo and them other Nose-Bones skin them Googerak. I never see a man skinned before. We don't do that in my old mob. They skin them Googerak from the waist down, then cook that skin in the fire. Daingumbo say they always eat the skin from the legs of their enemy. I say, this new to me, we don't do that in my mob. I say, in my mob we eat the fat round the kidneys of our enemy. I say this to Daingumbo and I think him true for old men in my mob always tell this to me, but I never do him myself. When that skin sizzled crisp, we all eat him. I not sure about eat Googerak, but got to if I Nose-Bone.

Them Googerak taste good. Better than bandicoot.

When Sun Woman rise we go more south, look for more Googerak. Sun Woman go over twice more, still we go south. Plenty wet country, plenty swamp. We come to end of Nose-Bone country, don't see Googerak. We go more south, into

Googerak country. Don't see Googerak. Don't see their fires, don't see their women gather tucker or grind seed. See their wurlies, see their camps, see their tracks, but don't see Googerak. Daingumbo say this as far south as he ever come. Then we smell bad stink come on wind. We go on proper careful.

That stink come from clearing near river. That clearing a Googerak camp place. That stink come from dead feller in camp. We go close, find many dead feller. We find dead woman, dead boy, dead girl, dead baby. All proper dead. They dead long time. Their bodies covered with flies and worms.

We find old men dead. We don't find any warrior dead. All these feller killed when their warriors not here.

"Who kill all these Googerak?" I ask Daingumbo.

He look troubled. "Not Nose-Bones," he say. "I don't see any feller killed dead like this before. Look, this one slashed with big cut, take off head. Like killed with sharp axe. We don't fight with axe. Don't know any mob fight with axe. Not right fight with axe. Many feller here killed by big cut. Look, see this baby, he cut in two pieces. Proper sharp axe do that."

Dead feller everywhere we look. So many dead feller, Daingumbo say all Googerak got to be dead except for their warriors. Perhaps their warriors still fight mob who kill their families.

That place a bad place. We all proper troubled. We look about for tracks. All that ground in camp proper churned up, many feet in fight. Then I see footprint like I never see before. I call to Daingumbo. He come over. I point to print, proper clear in earth.

We look at print. That print strange shape, like shape of twig bent for hoop. I think, this the footprint of man who have hoop for feet. Then we find more prints on trail to south of camp. We see they the prints of a beast with four feet. Each foot like twig bent for hoop. We see footprint of three of them beast.

I say to Daingumbo, 'I don't know this footprint, but my mob see strange footprint before. We see him to east of lake in north. That the footprint of beast with two heads. That beast footprint got no toes. That beast with two heads, he travel with man got no body.'

I proper scared. I remember how I scared when first hear of beast with two heads. I see Daingumbo troubled. I say to him, 'That beast with two heads kill clever man belong our mob. Cabba's dad point bone and sing that beast, kill him dead. I see body of that beast myself, he proper dead. Maybe these beasts friends of that beast with two heads, come back and kill all these feller avenge his spirit.'

I see Daingumbo more troubled. All them Nose-Bones troubled. We look around for more footprints, find plenty on trail out of camp to south. 'One thing more,' I say to Daingumbo. 'That beast with two heads got two tails drag on ground. This beast got no tail drag on ground.'

We follow that trail for a bit. He run down beside cliff. We go careful, keep good look out, but we still surprised by old feller who stand on rock high above trail. He got grey beard and thin hair like proper old feller. His beard and hair long like he got no woman singe them short for him. He stand on ledge in cliff. How he get there I don't know. He call down to us. He carry spear, but don't look like he throw. We put up our shields. He hold up fist.

We look up at him. He not Nose-Bone. He not Googerak. We don't know this man.

He call down in strange lingo. "Don't go on. You get killed dead, too right you do," he say.

Daingumbo laugh. "We Nose-Bone warriors! We don't get killed." He point at me. "This man got kangaroo cock. He never die in battle."

Old man nod like he know all this. He say, "You go on, you find plenty bodies of Googerak warrior who say same. Now they all dead. All them Googerak warrior proper dead. They killed by man-beast. Many man-beast south of here. They half man half beast. They got head of man and body of beast. They look at warrior, kill him with shout. They cut off heads and arms with sharp stick."

Daingumbo quiet at this. I know he not sure whether believe old man or not. I think, I give old man question, see what he know.

"Do you know of the man with no body?"

He look back at me, no smile. "Yes, them men with no body, they bad spirits. They live with man-beasts, run with them like dog run with us. They kill a feller dead with shout."

"Do you know of the beast with two heads?"

He look surprised. "I hear of beast with two heads, don't see. Man with no body live in belly of that beast with two heads!"

We quiet. This proper strange news. But we don't think old man mad, we think he know truth.

I ask him, "Do you know the feet of these man-beasts?"

"Yes!" he call back. "They got feet hard like stone, make print like bent twig!"

I say to Daingumbo, "This old feller tell truth. He know about all these things." Then I say to old man, "Where your mob?"

Old man give laugh, but laugh like sad laugh, not happy laugh. "I got no mob," he say. He don't say more. Maybe his mob throw him out for some reason. That happen.

I say to Daingumbo, we got to go back to Nose-Bone camp, protect wife and child. He say to me, hand of his father tell him same thing.

I think, maybe them Googerak we kill the last of them Googerak.

At Nose-Bone camp, all is good. Plenty tucker, plenty water. They don't see no Googerak, no man-beast. When we tell Nose-Bone mob all them Googerak dead, everybody happy. We have big feast, big dance, plenty good time.

I lie with Jinggaya in our wurly. Our wurly near wurly belong Daingumbo. We hear wife belong Daingumbo shout at him, tell him he gone too long, tell him he think too much about kill Googerak when he got to think about catch kangaroo for tucker! We crawl to edge of our wurly with big smile on face. We see wife belong Daingumbo by light of their fire. She shout, he do too much Goanna ceremony with other men when he got to get fish from river! She stand while she shout, Daingumbo lie on ground with arm over head. She shout, he go off with other woman, never have sex with her like husband should! She prod him with her yam stick every time she shout. He just lie there, say nothing. She tell him off proper good! She tell off good the great warrior Daingumbo!

Jinggaya and me we laugh proper silent see Daingumbo get told off. I say to her in quiet voice, 'I happy you don't tell me off like wife belong Daingumbo!'

She say with little laugh I like so much, 'I learn from Dilboong – that name of wife belong Daingumbo. I like her, she good woman. She strong, she happy. She keep that Daingumbo in order. She tell me I got to learn keep you in order, or you treat me bad like Daingumbo treat her!'

I laugh and give her stroke on back. "I never treat you bad, Malilba," I say. "But you shout at me like Dilboong shout at Daingumbo, you feel my waddy pretty damn hard on your backside!"

She throw back her head and by the light of our fire I see smile but same time she look like she fight back. With laugh in her voice she say, "I don't shout you, but you never quick enough for use your waddy on me, because I get you with my yam stick first!"

She say all this with laugh, but I think, yes, she strong woman, she don't put up with husband who beat her. I say, "Well, that Dilboong teach you good! But you don't want me lie on ground with hand over head, like Daingumbo?"

She stroke my neck and say in soft voice, "No. I don't shout you, Gunmyimbook, you good man. You treat me good. That Daingumbo, he don't treat Dilboong good. He tell you how he get his wife?"

"No."

"You see mark on his hand?"

"You mean that squash thumb?"

"No, he get that from waddy in fight with some feller. No, other hand."

I think. "Yes, he got mark other hand. Someone give him proper good bite, them teeth marks both sides of hand."

Jinggaya give her small laugh. "Them teeth belong Dilboong! She tell me all this. She come from mob in next country. Not Googerak, from mob to east. When she young woman, she out gather tucker when Daingumbo come down quick from bush and grab her. These Nose-Bones, that's how they get wife. She don't want leave her mob, don't want go with Daingumbo. He hit her on head with waddy. She grab him, bite his hand proper good, don't let go. She leave her mark on him for rest of his life! But he too strong for her, he hit her again. He carry her back to Nose-Bone camp while she too weak for fight. When she in camp, them Nose-Bones guard her, stop her from run back. Then she have baby, forget about own mob, decide stay with Daingumbo. She say he got much good in him, only little bit bad. Them Nose-Bones got their own ways."

I surprised. I say, "Now I understand why Dilboong tell off her husband! She proper angry woman. She brave, too, I think. She don't want anger Daingumbo too much. I think he lose temper, he hurt her proper bad."

Jinggaya say, "Yes, I think she know that."

I stroke her again. "I happy you get me with love-spell. I don't want hit you with waddy, get bite."

"Yes," say Jinggaya. "I don't want you hit me with waddy. I don't want shout at you. But I don't want you go off kill Googerak, either. I want you hunt kangaroo, spear fish, get good tucker, make good ceremony for Goanna, keep us safe. I got extra reason, now …"

"Extra reason? How you mean?"

She look at me with happy smile, same smile that make me feel strange when I first see her at that fireplace belong her father. "I think I got another baby inside me. I tell you that happen if we make camp near water."

*

Them seasons when Jinggaya grow big with baby inside her one of the best times of my life. Best time of her life, too, I think. Them Googerak don't come back, and them Nose-Bone don't go into battle. Still plenty fight between Nose-Bone feller, but that not scary like war with Googerak.

I hunt with my Goanna brothers. Not much kangaroo, emu in their country, got to go long way find that kind of tucker. But plenty fish, bird in all that wet land, and Nose-Bone women get plenty root grow in water. Them Nose-Bones got camp sites along the river. They don't follow the seasons like my old mob, they just move about a bit when the tucker get a bit low. They don't move far, so they don't leave their old feller behind when can't walk. They don't leave their injured behind like Mother Berangu. Their women can have two small baby. I glad their women can have two small baby, for new baby belong Jinggaya get left behind if born in my old mob, since Monanggu don't walk yet.

Jinggaya tell me time for baby come. She go off into bush with Dilboong and old Nose-Bone women. I

93

know I got to stay in camp. I see baby born when I boy. I hide in bush when woman drop behind our mob when we travel. She big with child, I guess she go have baby. I see her squat over trail, see baby fall into dirt, see that woman bite cord, clean up baby, pick him up then hurry catch up mob.

By and by Jinggaya come back with Dilboong. She got big smile, carry new baby across breast. Dilboong carry Monanggu. Jinggaya say, "Bradek, you got son."

I get up. I so happy, can't speak. Jinggaya pass me my son. He got baby face but skin wrinkled like old man. He got a bit of fair hair on his head. He got good hands, good feet, good cock. He got his eyes closed. He wriggle in my arms, start make noise. I give him back to Jinggaya and he quiet quick. I got a son!

I put hand round Jinggaya shoulder, touch baby with other hand. I tell Jinggaya she bring me a proper good son. I say, "What spirit give you this baby?"

Dilboong speak quick. "You don't trouble with that," she say. "Our clever feller find out what spirit your baby got. Now you got to get out, find some good tucker, feed your wife proper good so she can look after this baby!"

She point her yam stick at me as she say this, and poke him towards me. Her voice when she say this just like that voice she use on Daingumbo when she tell him off. I surprised. I look at Jinggaya with my mouth so open that yam stick can go right in him. Jinggaya look back at me. I see she surprised. Then I see smile in the corners of her eyes, and she start laugh, and then I start laugh, and then we both laugh proper loud. Dilboong don't know what make out of this, she don't know why we laugh. She get more cross and bang her stick on ground, but we laugh and laugh.

Later we go to Nose-Bone clever men find out what spirit enter Jinggaya, make baby. Them clever men say baby born at place where wombat leave shit. Spirit of wombat go into baby. They say my son name Nawngnaw.

Soon after Nawngnaw born, Dilboong get new baby too. Big trouble over this. Daingumbo and Dilboong already got four children. Nose Bone law say no one have more than four children unless grandparents say can. Daingumbo and Dilboong ask grandparents if they can keep this baby. Grandparents say no, too many children in mob, Daingumbo and Dilboong don't have more baby. One grandfather come to Daingumbo wurly, kill that baby by hit him across mother's knee. This their way. We don't have any way like that in my old mob, any baby got to die get left behind when mob move on. But them Nose Bones kill that baby by hit head on mother's knee. Then mother and father eat that baby after cook on fire, eat him for show their grief, eat him for remember him. We don't eat our own people in my old mob, but these Nose Bones eat their dead baby for remember them. They eat their old feller when die for remember them and get their wisdom. They eat their enemies for get their strength.

Dilboong sad long time after baby get killed dead, but my life good. I got Jinggaya. I got Monanggu. I got Nawngnaw. The Nose Bones have good dance, good feast. I go hunt for my family. Jinggaya get woman tucker. I make Goanna ceremony. Jinggaya make dilly, grind seed. I make spear point, make straight spear, carve coolamon. Jinggaya feed babies. All them things in our life good. Only one thing in my life not good. I don't tell Jinggaya about this. Some nights Cabba's dad come visit me when I lie in wurly. I lie there, I asleep, then I wake up and see this small man in darkness. He very small man. He always start very small. Then he grow, and I see him stand in entrance of our wurly. He carry shield and spear, he painted up for fight. He lower his shield, look over at me, and I see he Cabba's dad. I can't move. I can't move at all. Cabba's dad proper clever feller, he know how visit me in night, he know how make his *yowi* travel through spirit lands, reach my wurly. He know how stop me from make move. Cabba's dad stare at me with fierce look. He don't say anything. He shake his spear, then he stab him at me proper quick. That spear don't quite reach me. I know Cabba's dad show me what he do to me when we meet for fight.

In morning I think, do I dream about Cabba's dad? Do he come only in my mind? Then I look at entrance to wurly, and I know he stand there all right. He stand there, threaten me, give me trouble, then clear off. He wear grass on his feet so he leave no tracks. Then I think, Oh Bradek! You most stupid man on earth. You don't wear grass on feet when you run back from Berangu. Even though those tracks proper old, you know plenty feller in your old mob good tracker, can follow old track. Cabba's dad can follow any track, he get spirit help him when track faint. He follow track, find your wurly.

Then Daingumbo come to our fire and say, "Nantoomana, big mob come upstream. They say they your old mob. They say they come kill you for break their law. You got to go up there proper quick."

I get my shield and spears and waddy and go upstream with big crowd of them Nose-Bones. We travel fast but still got to make camp twice and stop get tucker before we get near the place my old mob camp. We get there soon after Sun-Woman get up in sky. I see him same place Jinggaya and me make camp when first come in Nose-Bone country. Already some Nose-Bone warrior stand in the bush, stop my old mob come further down stream. They say my old mob make camp other side of river, send message they want punish me.

Them Nose-Bones make a line our side of river. My old mob make a line other side. I surprised how many of my old mob come to that place. They make big line other side of river, but not as big as us line of Nose-Bones. That river, he proper small here, can wade across him easy. Them two mobs, they all painted up with white clay. I see plenty feller my old mob painted up with white clay and stripes and their totems.

We see that other mob do dance. I know that dance, I do him myself when we have big fight with Mairkaioo. I know that dance call on spirit of ancestor help kill enemy. Then Nose-Bones do dance. I don't know this dance, but I copy best I can. I guess this dance same like other dance. Them Nose-Bone men, they dance with knee bent, stamp both feet same time, proper quick. Got to be strong feller dance a lot like that. They show they strong feller.

When Sun-Woman high in sky, my old mob start a shout. I know that shout. He say, come brother, let us kill our enemy, let our blood run and let the blood of our enemy run. I tell this to Daingumbo. He say, Nantoomana brother of Daingumbo, all Nose-Bone fight enemy who invade Nose-Bone country. Then Nose-Bone men start a shout. He say, let us kill our enemy, let us eat the skin off his legs. And both sides shake their spears.

I think proper big fight start when one man step out in front of old mob line. I think, I know that man. He Cabba's dad. He look strong and fierce. I see other man behind him. I think, I know that man. He my own dad. Then I see behind him young men. Them young men Cabba and Borrudum. I happy see Cabba and Borrudum and I show myself to them. They don't do anything. I think, maybe they don't know me with bone through nose. They all painted up in white like men with grievance. Then behind line of men I see some women. I think, many of my old mob come over here after me.

Cabba's dad bang waddy on shield and shout out, "You Nose-Bones, we come for our son Bradek. He break the law, he run off with his mother-in-law! He got to be punished for break the law!"

Daingumbo come up to me. He ask, "That true? Black Cockatoo woman your mother-in-law?"

I think, I tell Daingumbo Jinggaya my mother-in-law he don't fight on my side. Then I think, I tell Daingumbo Jinggaya not my mother-in-law, he find out I trick him, he kill me. I think, I killed whatever I say. I don't know what say. I don't say anything.

"So this true then?" say Daingumbo. I sign yes, I sign can't help this. Daingumbo quiet. Then he say, "You got to fight on your own this time."

I say, "Yes, I know that. I fight one man against one man."

Daingumbo say, "I know why you run off with mother-in-law. That Black Cockatoo woman proper good woman. I run off with her myself if you don't!" He laugh. Then he stop laugh. "But you still got to fight on your own. My mob make sure this fight one man against one man, that all."

I show him I know what he say. Daingumbo and them Nose-Bones paint me up as accused man. They paint my face red all over. They paint stripes run from shoulder to breast-bone. They paint more stripes across my belly. All this paint say I accused man got to meet grievance man. Then I walk out in front of that line of Nose-Bones. Cabba's dad come nearer. I think, this bloody bad, that Cabba's dad best warrior in my mob. He kill dead Uncle Wugubu, cut off his legs. I look over my shoulder. Can't run away, big line of Nose-Bones there. Anyway, can't run away, got to face Cabba's dad.

When I look over shoulder, I see Daingumbo. He call out to me. He say, "Nantoomana! Remember! Grandfather Parangal say you never die in battle!"

I think, Yes! That true, Parangal say I never die in battle! That Parangal proper clever feller, he stop that point bone magic of Mairkaioo mob. I turn back towards Cabba's dad, stand up straighter, feel better. I know I got a small smile on my face, now I remember I can't die in battle. Cabba's dad see my smile, and I see that fierce look on his face change for one moment, him change into look which got trouble. Then he go back to his fierce look, and we walk closer. We still got that stream between us.

We stand for a bit, shields ready, keep good look out on spear thrower in hand of other man. I see Cabba's dad watch my spear thrower proper careful. I watch his spear thrower proper careful. We don't get no chance throw spear. No use waste a spear when man watch proper careful.

We keep same distance, step sideways downstream a bit, keep proper good look out. Then I hear footsteps run up behind me. I snatch glance over shoulder. Oh no! I think. Here come Jinggaya! Where she come from? She got to follow up behind Nose-Bone mob, leave babies with Dilboong.

Same moment I see Jinggaya, I see arm belong Cabba's dad lift up spear thrower and jerk him my way. His spear come straight at my chest. I see him and jerk my shield round proper quick. That spear hit that shield and glance off. That spear fall on ground.

At same moment great shout come from Nose-Bones. That Nose-Bone line run in closer. They shout, Nantoomana! They shout, Never die in battle! They shout, We eat the skin of our enemy!

Then Jinggaya got hold of my arm. She pull and scream. She scream, "No, Bradek! Don't fight Cabba's dad! He kill you dead! I don't want you get killed dead!"

I keep my shield up. I know Cabba's dad got another spear. Same time I try shake off Jinggaya. "Leave me!" I tell her. "You get me killed like this! Leave me!" But she hang on and I got to throw her to the ground. I throw her to the ground, but she get up on knees, then cling round my legs, then pull me back. She scream and shout proper loud. She scream all the time, everybody in both mobs can hear her scream. I know I got to keep my shield up to Cabba's dad but I know I can't do this while Jinggaya cling on to me. Then I see them Nose-Bones run in, they skim in throwing-sticks at Cabba's dad. He busy dodge them sticks. Them sticks fly round him like wagtails mob heron. He dodge and jump. I turn on Jinggaya and hit her with my fist on her face. I give her a proper mighty hit on the side of her face. She fall straight to ground. I see she still know what go on, but she hurt too much for move. I know she hurt bad, for my fist hurt bad. I hear her cry, and I feel proper bad about hit her. But then I see them Nose-Bones run out of sticks, and I got to defend against Cabba's dad again.

I run closer to him, leave Jinggaya behind on ground. We both in stream now, too close for throw spear. We circle proper careful. Then I see woman break through line behind Cabba's dad and run towards him. He see me look over his shoulder, and he put this thought in my head: I see you look over my shoulder, you pretend someone come up behind me, but I don't fall for trick.

That woman run closer, I see she quite old woman. She come closer, I see she don't run too good. When she proper close behind Cabba's dad, I see she Mother Berangu. Berangu live! I so happy, I forget keep shield up. Cabba's dad ready jab his other spear when Berangu shout out his name just behind him and put him off.

Cabba's dad turn quick. I see him forget keep look out one moment. I see his neck clear. I know one quick jab I put spear through neck belong Cabba's dad. I think about that, get spear all ready, but then don't jab. Why I don't jab I not sure. Maybe Cabba's dad use magic stop me throw. Maybe I don't want kill Cabba's dad dead.

Proper quick, Cabba's dad turn, keep look out again. I see he know I don't kill him. Then Berangu grab his arm, start shouting, 'No, no! Don't kill my son Bradek! No, no!" She shout and pull like Jing-gaya do me before, but now Cabba's dad keep his eye on me. He back off a bit, give side swipe with shield and knock Berangu to ground easy. Berangu got breath knocked out, she lie on ground crying.

Then Cabba's dad step closer to me. He just say to me, "You got to obey the law." Then he fix me with a fierce look and I see him the same look he give me at the entrance to our wurly. He keep look at me, and I find I can't move, same I can't move when he come to our wurly. Then he step closer and hold up his spear same he hold him when he come, and he jab his spear at me same he jab him when he come. And that spear go into my thigh. I see that jab but he don't hurt. I can't move. Cabba's dad pull spear back. I feel hot blood run down my leg. Still can't move. Cabba's dad back off, keep eye on me, but I can't attack him. I like turned to stone. He back off more, help Berangu get up, pull her back to line. I see her look back at me, that look got fright but got love too. I see her look back and I know she love me. I think back to her, I love you too, Berangu. I know she hear me.

Then I hear Cabba's dad call out to all my old mob, 'Bradek is killed! The law got to be obeyed! Now we go back to our own country!" I see that whole line of feller back up and vanish into trees. And I look at my wound and all that blood run and I think, yes, I killed, but I not killed dead.

In short time them Nose-Bones all round me. They say, you get killed but you not killed dead. They say, that warrior your mob can kill you dead easy. They ask, why he not kill you dead? Then they say, oh yes, he can't kill you dead because Nantoomana can't die in battle. And they say I got proper strong magic.

Now my leg hurt. I hold sides of cut together, try stop blood run. Then I limp over to Jinggaya, who still cry on ground. She in daze. I lie beside her, keep leg out straight. I turn her face to me. Her face covered in water from eyes. She got black bruise all round cheek. Jinggaya cry. I feel proper bad. I think, Bradek, you stupid! You most stupid man on this earth! You hurt that woman you love most on this earth! Now she hate you for ever! And I see Jinggaya look at me, and she look right into me, and she speak this inside my head: I love you, Bradek. And I feel that water come in my eyes.

I don't know who hurt more bad, Jinggaya or me. My leg cut wide open, deep cut with plenty blood run out. Jinggaya face swell up one side like burr on tree trunk. We both lie in grass near that stream, can't get up or move about.

Nose-Bone men get juice from bulb of white lily, rub in cut. They paint that cut with white clay, stop blood run. They get paper bark, wrap him round my thigh, tie him with grass keep cut shut. They sing medicine song for heal wound. That leg, him go all stiff so can't walk. They say can't do anything for Black Cockatoo woman. Then Dilboong and other Nose-Bone women come up from camp with

Monanggu and Nawngnaw, put them on breast of Jinggaya. Jinggaya don't like, her head hurt too bad, but can't help. Them Nose-Bone women get leaves of stinkwood plant, crush them leaves up, bind them round face belong Jinggaya. Them women sing medicine song for stop ache. Jinggaya sign this make pain less, but she still look bad. She don't like talk, make face hurt.

We lie there long time. Them Nose-Bones put branches over us, make fire near. They bring water and tucker. They put water in two skulls they put beside us. Now I know why Dilboong got them skulls. They better than coolamon for carry water, don't spill much. Jinggaya can't eat much, her jaw hurt too bad. Them Nose-Bone women chew up some of that tucker like for baby and give tucker to her that way.

Daingumbo come, say he ask Parangal how I get killed by Cabba's dad. Parangal say Cabba's dad put proper good spell on me. Parangal say he try put spell on Cabba's dad, catch his *yowi* when out in *dowi*, but can't, Cabba's dad magic too strong. Parangal say he break that spell Cabba's dad put on me, though.

Jinggaya lose her digging stick when she run after me. When I a bit better, I carve her a new stick. Daingumbo send me a good bit of wood, him a proper hard black wood, best can get for digging stick. Daingumbo send me good stone for cut wood. I carve that new digging stick for Jinggaya best I can, show her I proper sorry. I carve that black wood proper smooth, give him big club one

105

end, give him sharp point other end, make him flat in middle for good hold. I got plenty time make good digging stick. I carve middle of that digging stick. I carve Goanna and Black Cockatoo sign on that digging stick. I got plenty time make good Goanna and Black Cockatoo sign on that stick. When I finish, I give him to Jinggaya. She give me big smile even though he hurt bad. I proper happy get smile from Jinggaya.

We lie that place long time. I talk plenty with Jinggaya when she feel better. I ask if she sorry she run away with me. She say no. I ask if she angry I hit her. She say no. I ask if she angry I go to Goanna Rock for make ceremony. She say no.

I say, 'Why you got no ceremony? You Black Cock-atoo, why you got no Black Cockatoo ceremony? Why no woman got ceremony?'

She look at me like she don't expect this question. Then she say, proper quiet, 'You don't know?'

I don't like say I don't know. I keep quiet.

Then Jinggaya say, 'Us women, we don't need ceremony. We belong to this earth. Not like you men.'

I don't know what she say, but I don't like ask. I keep quiet more.

'Us women, we make life, same like earth make life. When we have baby we know how earth feel, we know we got spirit from earth inside us. We know we got to nurse that baby, nurse that baby like earth got to nurse all its creatures. We know we got to care for men, care for men like earth got to care for all its creatures. We know we got to leave baby yam, so earth can nurse that yam, make him grow so yam can feed men. We join to earth like cord join baby to mother."

I see she look at me. Her eyes big and kind. I feel the power of her caring. I still quiet.

"You men don't get this. You don't know what like be joined to earth. You got to make up for not be joined to earth. You got to make ceremony, sacred dance, sacred painting, sacred song, try join to earth. Us women, we already get that. We don't need them ceremony."

She never talk like that before. I keep quiet. I think then I don't know what she mean but now I think I know what she mean.

Later, she ask me if I happy in Nose-Bone country. I think. I think, some ways happy, some ways not happy. I think, maybe something wrong when we live with Nose-Bones, but I don't know what. I don't know how answer, so I say to her, "You happy in Nose-Bone country?"

She look at me long time. Then she say, "Their Dreaming not our Dreaming."

When she say this, I know she right. Too right, that Dreaming of them Nose-Bones not same Dreaming like my own mob, like own mob belong Jinggaya. I say to her, "What you want do? Where you want go?"

She say, "I want us go back to your own mob."

I say, "We go back to my own mob, Cabba's dad kill me again. Your dad kill you. We go back to my own mob, you can't carry Monanggu and Nawng-naw. We got to leave one behind."

I see that water come into her eyes and she cry proper quiet. She lie there while last light from Sun Woman fade on her face and she cry proper quiet. I think, Jinggaya, you unhappy woman. I think, Bradek, you most unhappy man on this earth.

*

That night I send my *yowi* to spirit of Goanna. I know how think my *yowi* through that *mulowil* now, can do him easy. My *yowi* meet spirit of Goanna, say "Goanna, this Nose-Bone Dreaming not my Dreaming. Got to go back to my own mob."

Goanna say, "Bradek, you can't go back to own mob. Monanggu, she full of spirit, she can't be left behind. That against the law. Nawngnaw, you make Jinggaya ready for his spirit, he your own son, he can't be left behind. That against him be your son. Soon he full of spirit too. You got to care for both them spirits."

I say, "Goanna, what can I do? Jinggaya not happy in Nose-Bone country."

Goanna say, "You got to wait until Monanggu can keep up in walk. Then Jinggaya can carry Nawng-naw when you hunt."

I say, "Goanna, you don't say Cabba's dad kill me again."

Goanna say, "You got to find that out for yourself. You got to ask Cabba's dad."

This hard. I don't do this before. I go search for *dowi* layer where live that *yowi* belong Cabba's dad. I get in wrong layer, this strange layer, I meet spirit of plants in this layer. Then in this layer I see spirit of Giant Yam. I think, Cabba's dad Giant Yam. I go to Giant Yam. I say, "Giant Yam, I look for Cabba's dad." That Giant Yam say nothing, he just show me a path all dark. I go down that path all dark. At end of path, I see *yowi* belong Cabba's dad. That *yowi* float in top of wurly belong Cabba's dad. I see Cabba's dad sleep on floor of wurly. He got fire smoulder at entrance, some smoke come in wurly. He got one wife sleep one side. He got other wife sleep other side. He got four children sleep near head.

That *yowi* run down into Cabba's dad. He wake up, and I see him look up at me. I say, "You kill me good in stream. I come back to my own mob, what happen?"

Cabba's dad say, "Yes, I kill you good in that stream. I punish you as law say. Maybe by and by you come back. You come back, you get worst site in camp. You get last choice from hunt."

Cabba's dad lie down and close his eyes. I think, his answer good, but what about Jinggaya? He know I think this, for he open his eyes quick and sit up again. He say, "That Jinggaya, she your mother-in-law. She got to keep the law too. She got to be punished by her own mob." Then he lie down and close his eyes again.

Then I feel the power of that *yowi* belong Cabba's dad. That *yowi* take hold of my *yowi*, blow him back down that dark path like strong wind drive bark canoe, shut him out of that layer. I know he don't let me in there again.

When we better we go down to Nose-Bone camp, stay there while Moon Man die and born again many times. Jinggaya face look same how look before. She ask me often how her face look, I say he look beautiful as ever. My thigh look a mess. I got big scar and cleft where spear go. Muscle all tangle round that cleft. Take time get that leg strong again. When I see that scar I think of punish by Cabba's dad. That punish stay with me rest of my life.

I hunt with Nose-Bone Goannas, but we don't go out hunt much, for we got lots of ceremony got to do in that place. I find out secret why them Nose-Bones got plenty fish all time. They got a net, they weave him like dilly bag out of string made from reed fibre. They get rocks, they put them rocks together proper close in that river like new river bank make river proper narrow. Big fish in that river can't get past rocks, got to swim alongside rocks to narrow point. Them Nose-Bones put net at narrow point, them fish swim straight into net. Them Nose-Bones get fish most days, don't need hunt much.

Jinggaya gather tucker with Dilboong and other Nose-Bone women every day. I tell her we don't go back to my mob until Monanggu can keep up. Jinggaya make Monanggu walk every day, make her strong for keep up. Monanggu play good with Nose-Bone children, she happy in that place, she soon learn run.

I say to Jinggaya, "Monanggu soon run like water hen. Maybe we go to my mob by and by! We got to hope you don't get more baby before Monanggu ready."

She look at me and laugh. That small laugh I like. She say, "Hope! We don't need hope!" She laugh again. "I sure I don't get baby."

I don't understand. "How you sure? Plenty water round here."

She laugh like trill of wren. "Don't you know?" she say. "When I due bleed, I eat plenty of that swamp rhubarb! He make me bleed good, don't get baby! All women know this."

I think, swamp rhubarb! Ugh! That swamp rhubarb, him make mouth dry up, him make tongue shrink. I feel hair stand up and back shiver from think about that swamp rhubarb. I say, "He stop you have baby all time?"

Jinggaya laugh like she think I stupid. I don't like

111

that laugh so much. Then she stop, and touch my arm. I like that touch, make me feel good. 'No, Bradek, not all time," she say. "You think of *talgi* thistle." I think, yes, now I remember. Ugh! That thistle worse than swamp rhubarb! Jinggaya say, "That thistle make woman dry up inside. Eat him long time, don't get more baby all time."

Then I say, "But not right season for swamp rhubarb. Swamp rhubarb all gone."

Jinggaya give me a smile. "That true," she say. "But clever women in these Nose-Bones cut him in season, then store him until next season. He don't taste so bad when dry, too."

I think, these women know many things I don't know.

*

Daingumbo and Dilboong have big fight. Dilboong say Daingumbo go with other woman while she out gather tucker. I know this true, but I say nothing. All camp know this true. No one know, maybe Dilboong don't get so angry. Whole camp know, she get proper angry. I know Dilboong go with other man too. I know this for Dilboong tell Jinggaya and Jinggaya tell me. Also, one evening after I go out of camp for shit Dilboong wait for me in bush when get back. I go secret place for shit, for got to bury all waste. Any man get my shit or my hair or any part of my body, he can use that bit put spell on me. I surprised find Dilboong wait in bush. She come up to me, she put hand on my cock, stir him up. He rise up, and Dilboong say, "Your cock flare out like kangaroo cock!" This true, because of slit in him. She say, "I want feel that kangaroo cock inside me!" I think then, I got to have sex with Dilboong, I want sex with Dilboong. I put my hands on her breasts. But then Jinggaya come in my head, and she say, "No, Bradek, I don't want you have sex with Dilboong, only have sex with me!" and I push Dilboong away and run back to camp.

All camp don't know this about Dilboong but all camp know about Daingumbo. Dilboong shout and scream at Daingumbo. Daingumbo squat at entrance to wurly, he roll reed fibre into string on his thigh. His children chew them reeds after make soft in fire, spit out fibre. Daingumbo say nothing. Then Dilboong put number one curse on him.

"You fall dead and let that blow-fly blow on your rotten flesh!"

This only woman curse, not strong like man curse, but this curse got to be answered. Man who don't answer this curse, he got shame. Daingumbo pick up bunch of fibre, add to string, roll string longer. He say nothing.

Dilboong get more angry. She shout and scream more. Her voice go all round camp. Daingumbo make no sound, he act like she not there. This make her mad. Then she put number two curse on Daingumbo.

'Sit there for ever! Sit there until the juice from your cock run red like blood!"

We know this curse, him a proper bad curse, he can make feller proper crook. Man curse same kind make woman fall dead. All camp watch what happen at Daingumbo wurly. We see this curse trouble Daingumbo. He don't look at us, don't look at Dilboong. He look at ground in front of him. He stop long time, do nothing. We all watch, say nothing, wait see what happen. Then proper careful Daingumbo pick up more reed fibre and roll that fibre into that string proper slow. He keep look at ground, say nothing. He got strong magic, that Daingumbo. That curse don't hurt him.

Dilboong go mad. She pull spears belong Daingumbo out of ground and throw them down. She pick up shield belong Daingumbo and throw him away. She pick up possum skin rug belong Daingumbo and throw him away. She pick up throwing stick and spear thrower belong Daingumbo and throw them away. She go pick up his waddy, which lie near him, but Daingumbo reach out quick and grab other end. Their children get out of way proper quick. She tug, he tug. She pull him over, but he hang on. Then she shout, "Leave this place! Go to that other woman! Take all your things with you! Go now!"

Daingumbo don't let go waddy, but he don't say anything either. Dilboong let go. She give a scream, pick up her digging stick and hit him on Daingumbo head. He jump up quick, take his waddy and hit at Dilboong. She fend off that waddy with her stick, but that waddy run down stick and hit her on arm. She jump in and hit that digging stick hard on Daingumbo head again. He

114

got blood run down face. He jump in and hit her on head with waddy. She got blood run down face. They hit each other more. They both got blood run into their eyes so can't see good, got blood run all down their bodies. Whole camp watch this. We think, one of them killed dead soon. They hit and hit, like take in turn. Then we see Dilboong tire of this. She throw down her stick. She fall on her knees and cover her face with her hands. She cry. Daingumbo see this and throw down his waddy. He grab Dilboong by hands and pull her into wurly. All camp hear them have big sex inside wurly, hear Dilboong cry out when get Daingumbo juice.

After, Daingumbo don't go with that other woman for a bit.

*

Monanggu can run and keep up. Jinggaya don't have more baby. I tell Daingumbo we got to go back to my old mob.

He say, "Why? You got all you want here. You got your Goanna brothers. You fight with us, you eat with us. Why you want go away?"

I don't like tell Daingumbo his Dreaming not my Dreaming. His Dreaming mean proper good lot to him, he think best Dreaming any man can have. He don't know my Dreaming.

I say, "I sad leave your mob, leave my Goanna brothers, leave you." I think of good reason. "But Monanggu and Nawngnaw got no grandfather, no grandmother in your mob. They got grandfather, grandmother in my old mob."

I see Daingumbo not sure about this reason. He say, "You got brothers here. Father and mother of them brothers, they grandfather and grandmother to your children by and by."

I sign him maybe. Then I think of other reason. "I born at Goanna Rock. That Goanna Rock proper sacred site. I got to paint Goanna sign there, got to make Goanna ceremony there. I do this alone, but better I do this with other Goannas from my old mob."

Daingumbo quiet some time. Then he touch me on shoulder and say in sad voice, "Yes, brother, you got to go back to your old mob. You know you can come back here if need."

When dark come we have big dance, say good bye to Nose-Bone mob. Their women sing sad songs. We all dance slow dance. Each one of them Nose-Bones in turn come to me and Jinggaya and say goodbye. Daingumbo say to me, "I lose a brother." Daingumbo say to Jinggaya, "I lose a sister." He say to Monanggu and Nawngnaw, "I lose a daughter, I lose a son." Then Dilboong come and say same things. Then I say to Daingumbo and Dilboong, "I lose a brother and a sister," and I say to their children I lose sons and daughters. Then Jinggaya say same things. We all got water in eyes think about lose all these feller. I lose brothers and sisters, I lose uncles and aunts, I lose sons and daughters. Proper sad lose all them feller. I think, these Nose-

Bones good to us. I think, these Nose-Bones fight a lot, they eat their enemies, they not like my old mob, but they good to us. I think, I sad go. I think, maybe I part Nose-Bone now. That part don't want go.

When camp asleep, before Sun Woman come, Jinggaya and me pick up all our things and walk off to our old country.

That journey take long time. Monanggu don't walk long and Jinggaya tire from carry Nawngnaw. Long part of that journey got no stream. Before Sun Woman rise in morning, we got to sweep all dew off grass into coolamon, make big drink. When no dew we got to dig root or find water some other way. We got to shelter from Sun Woman when she highest. We got to stop while Jinggaya give breast to children. When we come to that plain and that valley belong my old mob, we proper hungry and proper thirsty.

I see smoke up that valley. That smoke say, Bradek come back to our mob. He come back with his mother-in-law now his wife. He come back with two children.

Some feller from my mob come out meet us. Mother Berangu limp out first. She come up to me, touch my arm, say nothing. Then she smile at Jinggaya, wave hand bring her towards camp. Then she fuss over Monanggu. Then she look close at

Nawngnaw. She look at me and sign, this your baby? I sign yes. She sign, I very happy you have baby.

Then Cabba and Borrudum come. They stand a bit away, say nothing. I sign I pleased see them. They sign they pleased see me, but they don't come right up close, like they not sure about welcome me too much. I know then I still got to punish a bit for break law.

Nearer camp I see my own dad and my own mum. My dad stand there proper still, look proper stern. I look at ground. He don't say anything, don't sign anything. He still mad. But, I think, he don't shout me or kill me. My mum stand just behind him. She don't say anything, but she put this thought in my head: I pleased see my own son again and soon your own father forgive you if you behave good.

All camp stand or squat by their fires and watch as we come to middle of camp. Cabba's dad stand on one leg next to his wurly. He hold his spear. He say nothing. He just move his spear a bit, show me where I got to make my wurly at the bottom of the camp, outside all the good family wurlies, down where the cranky old men and loose women got to make their wurlies. I know this from when I visit him in *dowi*, I expect this. I show I know and go down to bottom of camp. There Jinggaya and me make our wurly, make our fire. We got to go long way for water, long way for fire wood. No one offer us any tucker, we proper hungry. We know we shamed. But we pleased be back in my own mob.

118

Mother Berangu soon come down to our wurly and sit at our fire. We glad see her. She look old and I think soon she don't keep up and got to be left behind when mob move on. She seem to know I think this, for she jump up sudden and do a little dance and say, "Look, I still strong and quick!"

Monanggu join in Berangu dance. Me and Jinggaya laugh. Then Berangu say she want talk with me alone. I send Jinggaya away with Monanggu and Nawngnaw, find some tucker.

Berangu say, "Bradek, I glad you happy with your woman. But you got to be proper careful, for them Mairkaioo want revenge. Husband of Jinggaya there, he want kill you dead. He come soon make big fight. Father of Jinggaya there, he want kill his daughter. He put plenty spell on her, make her sick."

I say to Berangu, "Mother, I don't fear husband of Jinggaya. I meet him in fight. Clever man in them Nose-Bones, he say I never die in battle. I know I win any fight with husband of Jinggaya."

Berangu look me a kind look. She say quiet, "Bradek, that proper good what that clever man tell you. But I know them clever man tricks longer than you do. Nose-Bone clever man say you never die in battle, that good. But if Mairkaioo clever man know this, he make spell break that spell of Nose-Bone clever man."

"How he do that?"

"Ai, ai," she say. "I don't know all them tricks of

them clever men, but they got plenty trick, plenty spell. Maybe they come with plenty spear, you dodge all them spear. But one of them spear they smear with grease from body of their ancestors. That powerful magic, make that spear strike home, can't dodge. They throw other spear, you dodge easy. Then they throw magic spear, you think you can dodge easy, but can't. That spear kill you dead."

I think, this old woman talk. But I love that old woman, so I don't tell her what I think. I say, "Don't worry, Mother, that Nose-Bone magic proper strong. I don't die in battle. That Nose-Bone clever man, he fly through air on magic cord, he fly faster than bird. He proper clever man."

Berangu look surprised. "He fly on magic cord? That proper clever." Then she look at me with question in her eyes. "You know Cabba's dad got magic cord too?" I sign no. "Yes, he got magic cord. He fly faster than bird. He fly to cloud, bring back water from that cloud. He fly to Mairkaioo camp or Nose-Bone camp, see what spell they make. He fly over hills, find where kangaroo rest up. He do all that flying with magic cord."

I don't know what say. I think, maybe Berangu don't know this, this just old woman talk. Then I think, no woman know about magic of Cabba's dad, that taboo, maybe Berangu make him up. But then I think, this old woman, she live in camp long time, she see Cabba's dad grow up, she learn plenty thing other woman don't know. Maybe Berangu know about magic belong Cabba's dad. But she know that magic, that dangerous for her. Plenty feller our mob kill dead any woman who find out about clever man magic.

Then Berangu say, "Don't tell anyone I say about magic cord belong Cabba's dad. I not supposed to know."

Now I think all she say is true.

I think, Cabba's dad got a lot of magic. I think, I need some of that magic, help me fight them Mairkaioo, help keep Jinggaya safe. I think, how I get that magic?

Berangu smile at me. I see she know what I think. "Yes, son, you need that magic. Too right you need that magic. You need that magic proper bad for keep Jinggaya safe. You know them Mairkaioo, they got plenty magic. They want put spell on Jinggaya. I know you hide any bit of hair or skin or shit belong Jinggaya so they don't get for spell. But that not good enough. Them Mairkaioo clever men, they use bone or gristle or fat or feather from any part of any water bird Jinggaya eat. They get that bit of that bird Jinggaya eat, they put spell on him, they put him in dilly and warm him with fat from body of their ancestors. When that fat warm that bit of bird, Jinggaya get sick in same part. If they get bit of beak, Jinggaya get sick in nose. If they get bit of wing, Jinggaya get sick in arm. If they get feather, Jinggaya get sick in skin. Any time Jinggaya eat water bird, you got to make sure all that bird burned up in fire, you got to bury any bit left over so them Mairkaioo don't find him."

This new to me. 'Only bird? Not fish or kangaroo?"

Berangu answer, 'No, only bird. No fish got any magic except when Jinggaya bleed, when can't eat fish. Kangaroo got no magic. But bird live in water, any kind of duck or heron or swan, got plenty magic."

I sign I understand what Berangu say. Then I say, 'But, Berangu, I got to get my own magic. I know how fight with spear or club. They come with spear or club, I fight them good. They come with spell, I don't know how fight spell. How I learn fight this magic?"

Berangu give me big smile. 'That easier than you think. Go see Cabba's dad!"

I surprised. I don't understand this. I say, 'See Cabba's dad! Why, Cabba's dad, he kill me over Nose-Bone way. Cabba's dad tell me sit down in this part of camp. Cabba's dad give me punish. Cabba's dad don't tell me any magic, he don't let his magic help me."

Berangu touch my arm. Her touch feel good. Some thought run out of her fingers into my arm and I know she know things I don't know. 'Son," she say, "go see Cabba's dad. He don't tell you this himself, but I know, for I know Cabba's dad from time he proper small, I see him grow, I know him when he made a man, I see him marry his wives, I see his children born, I know him become clever man by learn from Granddad Loolunar. I know I not supposed know all them things, but my eyes

122

always open, my ears always listen, my mind always hear all them thoughts around. I know that man, I know what he think. He think, that Bradek, he punish like law say. Now that Bradek punish like law say, no more punish. I know Cabba's dad don't want punish more. That Cabba's dad, I know he like his nephew Bradek. That Cabba's dad, I know he love his nephew Bradek. He know his nephew Bradek got good heart same like I know him, he know his nephew Bradek learn good. He see you can be clever man same like I see that. You go see Cabba's dad, ask him teach you all that clever stuff."

*

When Jinggaya come back, I tell her about water bird, tell her be careful when eat bird. She say yes, she be careful. She come back with root and grub, we cook in ash but still hungry when go sleep in wurly.

I don't like go see Cabba's dad, but that night I think, I visit him in *dowi*. I get to him easy. I say, "Uncle, I got to learn be clever feller like you."

He say, "Come first light to place where stones sit in circle." Then he push me out same like before.

When first light come, I go to place where stones sit in circle. Cabba's dad already there. He sign me squat on ground. Then he walk all round that circle, make sure no woman near. Them women not allowed near circle, but we know they try find out men secrets, they always listen or look if they can, we got to be careful all the time. After check, he come squat near me.

I don't like say anything about our fight, about Jinggaya. I say, "I come to you in *dowi*, uncle, ask you teach me clever feller things."

He sign yes, he know this. He say, "Bradek, nephew, you learn proper quick. You got power. I know that from way you learn travel that *dowi*. You learn clever feller things proper quick."

I glad hear this. Then Cabba's dad say, "Our mob don't know them Nose-Bones. We never go that way before. We don't know their magic. You learn any magic from Nose-Bones?"

I tell Cabba's dad about hand belong Daingumbo father. I tell him about kill Gugerak. I tell him about man-beasts and man with no body kill Gugerak. Then I tell him Parangal proper clever feller in that Nose-Bone mob. I tell him about take bone out of Jinggaya. Then I say, "That Parangal, he got most magic of any feller I know. He got magic cord. He can fly anywhere with that magic cord, faster than a bird."

Cabba's dad run his finger over his top lip. He seem not sure whether speak, not speak. Then he say, "I got magic cord, too. You want see him?"

I sign yes.

Cabba's dad reach in his dilly. He say, "First I got to make you ready see that cord. I got Rainbow Serpent here make you ready." He pull out kooderoo

shell. I think, I know that shell! He that shell
Granddad Loolunar show me when I made into
man. I know that shell, he got Rainbow Serpent
inside. Then Cabba's dad make that shell flash in
light from Sun Woman, and I see that Rainbow
Serpent! Cabba's dad say, "You see that Rainbow
Serpent?"

I say, "Yes."

"What that Rainbow Serpent look like?"

I say, "That Rainbow Serpent, he longer than a
man, he thick like my thigh, he green on top, he
yellow under, he got red wave all down body, he
got all them colours, he got head like kangaroo
head, he got ears like kangaroo ears."

Cabba's dad make grunt show he like this answer.
"That good, you see that Rainbow Serpent proper
good. You see clear what Rainbow Serpent look
like. Now I show you magic cord."

He put shell back in dilly and close him up. "That
cord in your dilly?" I ask.

"No. I keep that cord in my mouth. I keep him in
mouth all time, keep him safe, no one steal him.
Now I show you. I open my mouth and I pull out
that cord. Watch." He open his mouth and put his
finger and thumb in deep. He feel around a bit,
then he bring them out slow. They hold a cord! He
watch me all time. He pull that cord out a bit, then
take him with finger and thumb of other hand and
pull him out some more. He do this again and
again; he pull out that cord so he pile up on the

125

earth in front of him. Then the end of that cord come, and he put that end on the ground. "You see this cord?" he ask.

"Yes," I say.

"What he look like?"

"He thin and dark, like woman hair string," I say.

Cabba's dad grunt again. "Yes, he thin and dark, like woman hair string. But he strong as any cord you ever see. And he stretch further than any string you ever see. Watch! I throw end of this cord up into sky, he reach right up to that cloud! Look!" And he pick up end of that cord and throw him high up in sky, and I see that cord stretch out and fall over a cloud. That cord hang over that cloud so he stretch all the way from that cloud down to the ground.

I say, "That cord stretch right up to that cloud!"

Cabba's dad say, "Yes, he stretch right up." Then he laugh. "Now, watch good! You see me climb up that cord real quick. I come back with water from that cloud!" And he grab hold of cord and climb up him hand over hand real quick until he get to cloud, then he come back same way. When he back, he laugh and say, 'See! Here that water in coolamon! Drink!" And he pass me a coolamon full of water and I drink that water which taste fresh like rain. Then he say, "Now I put this cord away!" And he pull down that cord and put him back in his mouth. When he finish, I see no sign of that cord.

"Oh, uncle," I say. "This great magic! Can I ever learn this magic?"

"Yes, you can learn. You best learner of all young men in our mob. I know you want learn all them clever things. I teach you."

"Take long time learn use that cord?"

He laugh. "No! You learn proper quick. But other things you got to learn first. You come here every day, I teach you all them things. Each day you got to tell your woman you go hunting, but come here to me instead. You never catch anything hunting! Each day you got to tell your woman you don't catch anything. Your woman, your children, your own body, they all get hungry eat only woman tucker, but you got to do this. You come here every day first light. Moon Man torch grow thin then fat again. In that time, you learn all that magic!"

On way back to my wurly, I think, Bradek, you happy man! You happiest man on this earth! You learn all that magic from Cabba's dad! You proper clever man!

Each day I go to that place where stones sit in circle. Each day Cabba's dad show me things clever man got to know.

First he show me how make medicine for sick people. He show me how chew up root of reed or mallee leaf for cure sore throat. He show me how smoke a feller over green leaf fire for cure skin sickness and bad joints. He show me how break up bad blood in a feller by brush him with feathers greased up with fat from dead ancestor body. He show me how bleed a feller when blood got to be let out for let out pain. He tell me song I got to sing for different sickness.

Next he show me how make rain come. He don't show me all of this, for we don't want more rain just then. He show me which rain shoot I got to break. He show me most of that ceremony and sing me the song but just tell me other bits so rain don't come right away. He show me how make rain stop when too much.

He show me how kill woman dead with no one know how. He show me how kill man dead with no one know how. He show me how use little finger get fat from round kidney of any feller even when he alive.

After a bit, he show me how suck out blood from inside a feller who got sick lung or sick belly. I see this done before, I see clever man suck that part and spit out plenty blood. First he put woman hair cord over sick man, cord smeared with grease from dead ancestor. Then he suck out bad blood. Cabba's dad show me how clever man got to bite his cheek or cut his gum when he suck that sick part, then spit out own blood, and say to feller, "Look, I suck out all that bad blood in you, now you get better."

I say to Cabba's dad, 'I spit out my own blood, then? Not the blood of that sick feller? This just a trick, then?"

Cabba's dad look at me and say, "You see this done before. Does that sick man get better?"

"Yes," I say, "he get better," for sick man cured by clever man suck blood always get better unless he put under spell from some other clever man.

"Not trick, then," say Cabba's dad. "That bad blood in that sick feller, he sent by hair cord into your blood so you can spit him out."

Later he show me how take stone out of feller got stone inside him. Maybe stone put there by spell of enemy. He show me how get feller look away, how get stone from dilly bag, how keep him secret, make that stone seem come from sick feller belly. "That stone don't really come from sick feller then?" I ask.

"Yes, he do," say Cabba's dad. "The stone inside that sick feller sent by hair cord into stone in your hand. You got to have stone in hand, and he got to know he see stone from inside him, so he know that sickness cured. No trick. He get better, don't he?"

I got to agree, he get better.

I learn plenty more clever man things, then Cabba's dad say, "Tomorrow, I show you how go up to cloud on magic cord."

*

When I get to place where stones sit in circle, I see Cabba's dad there and I see Borrudum there too. Cabba's dad sign me squat beside him. He look

129

right in my eyes and he say, 'Bradek, nephew, you see all that happen here, but you don't see all that Borrudum see. And you say nothing, whatever happen." I don't know what he mean by this, but he sign me not ask.

Then he turn away and face Borrudum. He show Borrudum that magic kooderoo shell same he show me. He say to Borrudum, 'Look in this shell. This shell got a Rainbow Serpent inside him." And he make that shell gleam in light from Sun Woman. I see that light go up and down over eyes belong Borrudum. 'You see that Rainbow Serpent?" ask Cabba's dad.

'Yes," say Borrudum. 'I see him."

'What that Rainbow Serpent look like?" ask Cabba's dad.

'He long and big, he yellow all over, he got big green tongue flick out," say Borrudum.

'That right," say Cabba's dad. 'You see that Rainbow Serpent good. I put him away in my dilly. Soon I show you magic cord. You see magic cord before?"

'No, I don't see him before."

'I keep that magic cord in my mouth," say Cabba's dad. 'He keep safe in my mouth, where no one steal him. Now, watch me pull him out of my mouth." And I see again Cabba's dad put his finger and thumb right in his mouth and feel around, and I see him pull them out like they pull out cord. But that cord not there. I see nothing come from mouth belong Cabba's dad. But he take finger and thumb of other hand and make like they pull on cord. But that cord not there. And he keep do this until like end of cord come and he make like drop end on ground. But I see no cord on ground.

Cabba's dad point to ground and say to Borrudum, "You see that cord?"

"Yes," say Borrudum.

"What he look like?" ask Cabba's dad.

"He long cord, rough like cord make from reed fibre," say Borrudum.

"Yes," say Cabba's dad. "He rough like reed fibre, but he stronger than any cord and he stretch further than any cord. Now! A cloud come in the sky right over your head! You see him?"

Borrudum look up. "Yes, I see him," he say. I look up. I don't see any cloud in sky.

"Watch!" say Cabba's dad. "See me pick up this cord and throw him over that cloud up in sky!" And he stand up, make like he pick up one end of that cord in one hand and throw up all the rest of that cord with his other hand, and he stand and look up at that cloud. "You see that cord hang over that cloud and stretch down to the ground here?"

"Yes," say Borrudum.

"Now you watch good," say Cabba's dad. "You see

131

me run up that cord, go in that cloud and come back with coolamon full of water from that cloud. Watch!" And I see Cabba's dad make like he climb a cord, hand over hand, but he stay on ground. But I see head of Borrudum turn up to sky like he watch man climbing. Then I see Cabba's dad make like he fill coolamon, then make like he climb down. He go over to Borrudum and say, "Now I back on ground with coolamon. Drink!" And he make like he pass coolamon to Borrudum, but I see nothing in his hand. Borrudum make like he take coolamon, make like he drink. I see his throat swallow, and he say "Ahh!" and wipe mouth like he have good drink.

Cabba's dad say, "Now I put this cord away," and he make like he pull down cord and push him back in his mouth. When he finish, he say to Borrudum, "Now, when I sit down, you go back to your fire like normal man. You remember everything you see here, but you tell no woman or child. When you leave this place where stones sit in circle, you forget you see Bradek here."

Cabba's dad sit down. Borrudum stand up and walk off.

After Borrudum go, Cabba's dad show me clear how he make Borrudum see all them things he want him see. He trance him. I know I promise tell you all good truth, tell no lies, but can't tell you all this, could be bad. Cabba's dad tell me, "Hard trance feller not ready. But I trance any feller our mob easy. I trance them all, make them ready see things many time before. Granddad Loolunar make them ready many time before that. Every feller our mob ready. Only clever men know how not be tranced."

I squat beside him, say nothing. I think hard, think back to strange things. He pick up some of my thought. "Yes," he say quietly. "That time we fight in Nose-Bone country, I tell you stand still, get my spear in your thigh. I tell you he don't hurt much. You know I can kill you dead then, but you good feller, you don't kill me when Berangu run up, so I don't kill you dead. I know you make good clever man, but I got to punish you like law say."

I still quiet. I got too many thoughts in head, my head hurt and I don't see clear. Then I say, "That clever man of Nose Bone mob, that Parangal, how that old man get to our wurly before all the young men who run before him? How he do this by fly on magic cord?"

Cabba's dad smile at me. "I can do that," he say. "You can do him too, by and by. That Parangal, he got same kind of magic. He get to wurly after you. But when he get there, he trance you and he trance all them feller with you, tell you he get there first. After, that all you know."

Now my head hurt proper bad with all them thoughts.

*

Borrudum go all round camp, tell men how he see Cabba's dad climb up magic cord into cloud and get water. He don't tell woman or child. He come to my fire in evening, call me away from Jinggaya,

133

and he tell me what he see. He don't know I there. All men in that camp, they know Cabba's dad got powerful magic. I know too that magic proper powerful. I think, maybe I try some of that magic now Cabba's dad show me how. I say to Borrudum, 'Borrudum, come here, I got something show you." He come over, look at my hand which I close like fist. I open him up and show him quartz crystal. Late in day, Sun Woman go down, but that crystal he still glow, he glow orange and red from Sun Woman light. I rock that crystal and do other things Cabba's dad show me. Then I say to Borrudum, 'Borrudum, you look in crystal, you feel good, he make you feel sleepy, you feel like fall asleep." And I see Borrudum yawn. Then he lie down on ground and fall asleep!

Then I say, 'Borrudum, when you wake up, you want share your meat with me and Jinggaya. You don't remember I say this. You wake up soon, you don't remember what I say, you want share any meat you got. You share him with me and Jinggaya. You feel good when wake up. You wake up now!"

Borrudum wake up. He look at me and smile. He say, 'Bradek, my brother, you got no meat! I got kangaroo cook in my fire. You my brother, Bradek, you and Jinggaya come to my fire now, you chose which bit of that kangaroo you want!"

Now I know the power of that magic belong Cabba's dad, and I know I learn that magic good.

*

Jinggaya away search for tucker, so I go alone to fire of Borrudum family. They already eat lots of that kangaroo, but got some left. I hungry for meat, I eat him like starving dog! All them family belong Borrudum, they laugh see me eat so hungry. I don't mind this, we all laugh together and I glad for that company. They talk to me and make jokes round the fire and I think, at last I proper glad be back with my own mob. From things they say, I know some of them know I got Cabba's dad as teacher, and I see they treat me good for this. We all sing the song of our mob and I feel good.

When I get back to my wurly, Jinggaya there with woman tucker. I send her over to fire of Borrudum family while I play with Monanggu and Nawng-naw. I have good time with them children, they excited, they run and scream. I chase them round camp, make like I not fast enough catch them. I hide behind bush when dark, jump out when they don't know I there. They laugh a lot. We have good time, don't seem right any bad thing happen. But that night three bad thing happen.

One bad thing happen. Cabba's dad come by, he say, "Bradek, feller come from Mairkaioo with message stick. He got three rings on arm. He say husband of that Black Cockatoo woman challenge you to ordeal. They come soon, give you ordeal."

I stand up, beat my chest. "Huh! That husband treat Jinggaya bad! He beat her! He too old and slow fight me himself, so he want ordeal! Well, send message my Goanna keep me safe in ordeal, and after put curse on Mairkaioo!"

I know what they want from ordeal. Them Mairkaioo men stand off in line, throw all their spear at me. I get hit, maybe I killed dead. I don't get hit, ordeal finish, they don't trouble me again. I good at dodge spear, I feel good about ordeal. Parangal say I don't die in battle. Then I remember what Mother Berangu say. Maybe one of them spear smeared with grease from ancestor, maybe one of them spear got strong spell and reach me. That messenger got one ring for each day travel, so them Mairkaioo three day away.

Another bad thing happen. Granddad Moyana and Uncle Yawingaba come run through camp. They come back from hunt many days. I see they look troubled. "What trouble you?" I call as they run up. "Why you run?"

They stop near me. Yawingaba speak "We come up from south. We in creek, watch for kangaroo. Then we hear shout like thunder downstream. We go look. We find track of four leg beast. That beast got no toes. We follow that track. What we see ... we never see beast like that before. He proper big, tall like two men, some of him like man but he got giant body and four legs and he run over the flat faster than any man run. He shout again like thunder. We see kangaroo fall dead at shout. Moyana say we got to come back here quick, tell Cabba's dad."

"The man-beast!" I say. "That man-beast, he proper dangerous beast. I see what man-beast do to enemy of Nose-Bones over Nose-Bone way. That man-beast, he kill all the women and children in camp, he cut baby in half with axe, he cut off head with axe. That man-beast, he most dangerous beast. Run! Tell Cabba's dad proper quick. We need proper strong magic fight that man-beast!"

Other bad thing happen. As Moyana and Yawingaba run off, Jinggaya come back from fire of Borrudum family. She run up, say 'Oh Gunmyim-book, I don't like. I see one uncle from my old mob, he come as messenger. He see me at Borrudum fire, give me bad look."

I say, 'Cabba's dad come, tell me that message come from Mairkaioo. They want give me ordeal. I say, tell them come! I fight any ordeal!" I see Jing-gaya troubled. 'Don't be troubled,"I say. 'I safe in ordeal. Remember, Parangal say I never die in bat-tle. I safe, and after maybe they don't trouble us more." I give her comfort stroke. "At least you get some meat at last."

'Huh!" she say. 'That kangaroo all finish when I get there. All they got is cormorant. I hate cor-morant, he taste like bad fish."

'Cormorant?"I say. 'Cormorant a water bird."

'So?" say Jinggaya. I see she don't know what I mean.

"You eat any of that cormorant?"

'Only a little bit. I say, he taste like bad fish."

'That uncle see you?"

137

Now I see she know what I mean. She look proper troubled. "Oh ... yes, I eat when he see me."

"What happen to rest of cormorant?"

"I ... I leave him by fire."

I run over to Borrudum fire, find that cormorant. I find wings of cormorant, legs of cormorant, body of cormorant.

I don't find head of cormorant.

My Jinggaya get head ache. He not too bad at first. I give her medicine I learn from Cabba's dad, she feel not too bad. But third day she get fever. She don't sleep at night, she troubled, she move all time, she shiver like leaf flap in wind. When morning come, she like she don't know where she lie, she don't know who sit beside her. I get Cabba's dad come to our wurly, find her trouble.

He don't look long before he say, "This woman sick from some spell."

I say, "Uncle, I fear that. Jinggaya eat cormorant when messenger come from Mairkaioo. After, I don't find head of that cormorant."

"Aah," say Cabba's dad. "Clever man in them Mairkaioo get that head. He put him in dilly, warm him in ancestor grease. I know that magic. He proper powerful magic. More warm that cormorant head, more sick your woman. I think she die by and by."

Them words hit me like blow from waddy. I say, "But, no way we undo that spell? Don't you have spell cure Jinggaya?"

He sign no. "This powerful magic. I can't fight him. Only one way cure Jinggaya. That get hold of that cormorant head, put him in water, cool him down."

I think, how I get hold of cormorant head? "Uncle, can I creep into wurly of clever man, steal his dilly while he sleep and get that head?

He say, "Nephew, no. Can't do that, too hard." Then he look at me and say, "Wait."

He squat with arms round knees. He close his eyes like he sleep or think hard thought. I watch. He say nothing. He sway back and forward a bit. He like this long time. I think, he fall asleep? But I don't like wake him up. Then he let go his arms and open his eyes quick.

"No, son, that too hard. That clever man, he listen all time, he like quail in grass watch out for eagle. You get near his wurly, you get troubled. When you troubled, he see your *yowi* easy, he know you come. He wake up, meet you with spear!"

I sad hear this. I think, I got to find *some* way cure Jinggaya. I say to Cabba's dad, "Uncle, can you trance me so I don't get troubled thought when near that clever man wurly?"

He look at me. I see he think. He speak quiet and slow. "Maybe. Maybe I can. We don't talk about that now. Today them Mairkaioo come, give you ordeal. You got to come with me now, I get you ready for that ordeal."

That ordeal! How I hate him. But I know I got to go through that ordeal. I don't go through that ordeal, them Mairkaioo take revenge on all my family, they kill my father and mother and my brothers and sisters.

"How you know them Mairkaioo come?" I ask.

"I smell them! Don't you?"

I think, yes, now he say this, I do.

*

All them Mairkaioo line up other side of the flat near our camp. Our mob line up our side. I keep out of sight behind our line. Them Mairkaioo make big song. They stamp feet in dust. They call out, "Bring out our enemy, Bradek, who steal his own mother-in-law, bring him out so we avenge this!"

Our mob call back, "Bradek comes. Mairkaioo spear too slow catch Bradek! Mairkaioo can't throw spear straight! Mairkaioo can't spear lame wallaby!"

When they all fired up I run through our line and stand up tall in front. Them Mairkaioo go quiet when they see me. They don't expect see me how I look then. I hear them gasp, hear them say, "What

that?", "What this magic?" I see them look troubled.

Cabba's dad get idea dress me in emu feather. He
tie emu feather round my ankles. He tie emu
feather round my wrists. He tie emu feather to my
head. Now I look tall and big in them feathers.
Cabba's dad say to me, 'With these feathers you
run and jump like emu. No spear hit you, you see
spear from long way off, them spear come slow like
only weak man throw him." He ask me for my
shield. I pass this to him. He take something from
his dilly and smear a spot on that shield. 'This the
grease of Granddad Loolunar," he say. 'This the
most powerful grease we got. This grease save you
from magic of other mob!"

Moyana paint me up as accused man. He give me
that red face and stripes. He also paint Goanna sign
on my chest in red ochre so Goanna help keep me
safe in ordeal.

My idea put bone in my nose. I like that bone, he
look good, he make me look fierce, he trouble my
enemy. They don't see bone like that. I like wear
that bone like Nose-Bone feller, remind me Grandfather Parangal say I never die in battle. Them
feathers, that painting, that bone … them
Mairkaioo don't see man like that before.

When I stand at front of that line and all them
Mairkaioo go quiet, I beat my chest and call out in
loud voice, 'I Bradek! Black Cockatoo woman come
with me of her own wish! Your spear don't come
near me!"

One spear come from their side. He come slow, so slow, slow like leaf fall from tree. I see him long way off. I watch him good. I got time move one side. I move a bit, let that spear pass through feathers on leg.

More spear come. They all come slow, slow like seed fluff drift on wind. I see them come good. I dodge this one, hit that one away with my shield, jump over other one. I dodge, hit, jump more. Many more of them spear come, but they come so slow, like flight of pelicans land on lake, they easy dodge, hit, jump. Them spears go through my feathers, they go under me, they go over me; they don't come near me.

Now him rain spears. They all come slow, like pollen drift down from tree in still air. I laugh. This like a game I win easy. All them spear come, I hit one this way, one other way, jump over this one, duck under that one, jump one side, jump other side. None of them spear hit me.

Then I see one spear come fast through all this rain of spear. That spear, he go high like eagle soar in sky, then he rush down on me like eagle dive on dove. That spear come fast, come past all them other spear, head straight for me. I think, I know this spear. This that spear they grease with fat of dead ancestor, this that magic spear that kill me. I see that spear rush down on me and I know this spear don't miss.

At last moment I jerk up my shield. That spear, he thud into my shield. That spear, he thud through my shield! I see his point come through my shield. His point come between my fingers where they hold that shield. His point hit that patch of grease from Granddad Loolunar that Cabba's dad put on front of shield. That spear hit my shield but he don't hurt me! That grease of Granddad Loolunar save me!

This spear knock me off balance and I fall back. I hear great shout from Mairkaioo. I know they think they kill me. Some other spear still come. I watch them, hit them away with that spear that stick out of my shield. Then I jump up, shake my shield at them Mairkaioo and let out a shout. I beat my chest and run about, show I alive. All them Mairkaioo go quiet. I hear a big noise come from their side, noise like groan and grunt. I know they beaten. They got no spear left and I still run about.

Then all them feller in my mob start shout. They shout, 'Bradek live! Mairkaioo throw spear worse than woman throw spear! Go back to your camp!' They all stamp ground, shake their spears and shields. They all glad see me beat them Mairkaioo. For short time I think maybe big fight break out both sides, but soon them Mairkaioo walk off down their way. Soon they all gone. I not got to fear Mairkaioo any more!

All my mob run up to me, say they glad I beat them Mairkaioo, say I got strong magic, say I now safe from that Mairkaioo revenge. Cabba's dad come up to me, he say, 'Bradek, you show you got strong magic. Time you move your wurly up in camp, near wurly belong your father!' I so happy hear

143

them words.

They all go to big dance and feast. I go, but Jinggaya not there. I go to my wurly at bottom of camp, tell her good news. She there with Mother Berangu, who bathe her head. Jinggaya look a bit better but she don't talk.

Berangu say, 'She feel a bit better because Sun Woman go down, make air cool. That cool air make dilly of that clever man cool, cool down his magic. Tomorrow, when Sun Woman come again and warm that dilly, Jinggaya pain come back strong.'

I say to Berangu, 'I got to stop that clever man magic.'

I say to Jinggaya, 'What that clever man belong your mob look like? Where he build his wurly?'

Jinggaya roll her eyes, try to speak, but can't. Mother Berangu answer my question. 'I know that clever man. His name Muluru. He my nephew in that mob. I dream father belong Jinggaya go to that clever man for spell. I see him go to Muluru, say his daughter run away with her son-in-law. That Muluru say that against law, that a crime mob got to punish. Yarrungaitj say 'You got to make spell kill that daughter of mine dead.''

Berangu look up at me. 'That Muluru, he odd man, he got no hair on top of head. His skin crease all down sides of his body, like creases in caterpillar.'

'How I find his wurly?'

Berangu sign she don't know. She look troubled. "Why you want know that?"

"I got to find his wurly, get that cormorant head from his dilly. I know this the only way save Jinggaya."

"Ai, ai," say Berangu. "Them Mairkaioo catch you, they kill you dead! You risk get killed dead for save Jinggaya?"

I sign yes. "This the only way."

Berangu sigh. "You got to love that woman a lot," she say.

"I do, Mother," I say. "I love you, too. I think about you, I think about feel warm, feel happy, feel good. I think about Jinggaya, I think hurt inside. That how I love her."

Berangu laugh. "You love her good, then! You love her good and bad!" She laugh more. I like see Berangu laugh. Then she touch my arm. "You know them Mairkaioo, they my old mob, and they old mob of your own mother. I can go down their camp, see my brothers and sisters. I can go down there, come back, tell you where Muluru got his wurly. If that what you want."

I think, you love me good, Berangu. Can I ask old woman walk three days to Mairkaioo camp and three days back? Maybe Berangu don't have much walk left in her. But then I think, what else I do? I got to find that clever man. Only way save Jinggaya.

I look at eyes belong Berangu. They smile at me. I smile back, and sign thank you.

I run to Mairkaioo country three days after Berangu leave. I follow her track. When I near that Mairkaioo camp, I hide in bush, keep watch.

Before I leave own mob camp, I go see Cabba's dad, tell him my plan. I say, 'I want you trance me so I don't think troubled thought near wurly of that clever man."

He make long breath come out. Then he say, "All right, I do that."

I wait for him say or do more. He do nothing. 'I ready," I say.

He smile. 'I do him," he say.

"Go on, then," I say. I wonder why he fool with me.

'No, you don't understand," he say. 'I do him already."

He right, I don't understand. 'When you do him?" I ask.

'Right now, I do him. You don't know him now. You forget. That all."

'I forget?"

He sign yes.

I think, how I forget that short time? I can't forget. I think, he don't trance me. He don't want trance me or he can't trance me. Now he just trick me. I angry. I hide my anger, I don't want upset Cabba's dad. I hide anger, walk off.

Now I wait in bush near Mairkaioo camp. I know I got purpose, but I don't remember that purpose. I proper calm. I keep still in bush, keep good look out. Sun Woman go low over trees. I keep so still in them trees, bush wallabies come round feed near me. I don't move. Them wallaby nibble like I not there. They look at me but don't see me. I think, I can't make noise go after them wallaby. They come nearer. They right beside me. I think, them wallaby too good to waste! I jump out and get two of them easy with my waddy. I don't like make noise, but them wallaby wait to be got.

When all quiet again, a voice come through trees. "That you, Bradek?"

I shocked. That voice woman's voice. I think no one know I there. I think, who that voice belong to? "Who is there?" I call.

A laugh come back. "Why, your Mother Berangu, of course. Who do you think?" Now she speak normal I recognise her voice. She step from behind tree.

I say, "Mother Berangu! I wait for you here long time."

She say, "I know! I leave Mairkaioo camp long time back. Then I feel some feller watch track. I don't

147

know you that feller. I scared get watched, so I hide in trees, creep up slow, find out who there. When you get them wallaby, I see you clear."

I think, Bradek, you stupid, you let old woman creep up on you. You don't know she there. You call yourself a hunter! 'How you get so close, me not know?' I ask.

She laugh again. 'I old woman, Bradek. I learn lot of tricks in my time. I learn how be patient, take time, wait. When two feller hide in bush, one who most patient don't give himself away. That strange thing: old woman, not got much time left, can be patient; young man, got plenty time left, can't wait."

I laugh too. Then I say, "You find wurly of that clever man?"

"Yes," she say. "That Muluru, he helper to number one clever man belong Mairkaioo. That Muluru, he got wurly north side of camp under she-oak. He odd, that man, he got no hair on top of his head, he got crease like caterpillar down side of body. I damn sure he make spell on your woman, I see in his eyes he make that spell. I kill him myself if I not such old woman."

I give one of them wallaby to Berangu, ask her share him with Jinggaya. She go off to our camp. Then I tie grass to feet and creep closer to Mairkaioo camp as last light of Sun Woman go. I see their fires through the trees. I see them eat; that make me proper hungry. I hear them sing the song of their mob. While they sing, I creep proper quiet to north of that camp. When I get to that north side, I see wurly under she-oak. Big fire burn near that wurly. Two women bring wood for that fire. I think, these the wives of Muluru. Then man come out of wurly. He odd feller, he got no hair on top of head. The light of that fire show me he got creases down side of body. That light make deep shadow like black stripes painted down body. He bring out dilly and put him near fire. I think, he warm that cormorant head make my Jinggaya sick! I think, I put my spear through his throat now! When I think this, he look up and look about like he hear my thought. I think, not yet, Bradek, you spear him now that whole mob come after you, kill you dead, too right. I think, you keep calm, Bradek, you learn from Mother Berangu, you wait patient, wait for your chance. And I think my mind go empty of thoughts and I wait patient and watch.

I see that odd feller eat woman tucker. I see his wives go down toward corroboree. That odd feller, I think maybe he go down after eat. I see him finish that woman tucker then he lie down outside wurly. This part of camp all quiet. I watch, listen, don't move. I see no one.

I creep a bit closer, right to edge of bush which come up to camp. Now I hear that odd feller snore. I know this mean his *yowi* out in that *dowi*. He snore good. He lie on his back, face to the stars, and he snore good as his fire warm him and that dilly sit between him and that fire. I think, while that man snore, I creep up and take his dilly!

149

I got to come into open get near. I keep low, move very slow, creep this foot that foot over toward Muluru, all time keep look out in shadows. I listen good, but only sound of that corroboree come up from further down camp. I creep more. Then I think, this good! I don't think no troubled thoughts! I calm! Maybe Cabba's dad put that trance on me good after all.

I get up closer to Muluru. I careful my moon shadow don't fall on him. Not much wind, but I careful my smell don't carry to him. I got spear. I think, do I spear Muluru to ground, grab dilly and run? Or grab dilly and then spear Muluru? Or grab dilly and don't spear Muluru? I think, I spear Muluru to ground, them Mairkaioo find my spear, they use him for put spell on me. So I think maybe I just grab dilly. Then I think, that Muluru, he try kill Jinggaya, he try with bone and now he try with water bird head. I don't kill Muluru, he try again. That Muluru, he got to be killed dead.

I creep past Muluru toward dilly. I reach out for dilly when I hear snoring stop. I turn, see that feller head come up and his eyes wide. They gleam at me in the fire light. I see my shadow from fire light pass over that feller, wake him up. But he not full awake, he not sure what go on. I leap high in air, jump like kangaroo, land with both knees on that feller chest, knock all the breath out of him before he can call out. Then I get both my hands round his throat, squeeze that throat tight so he can't get more air, can't make noise. He don't struggle much. I think, why he don't struggle much? Maybe he got too little air for struggle. Then I feel his hands come up over my shoulders, proper gentle. I think, why this dying feller want stroke my shoulders? That don't save him. Then I think, this man a clever man like Cabba's dad. He know all them tricks of clever man. He know how kill a man dead by find secret place on his neck, same like Cabba's dad show me. That what he try to do now! I kick myself up with my knees quick, same time flap my elbows like bird wings, knock away his arms, then I land both knees on his shoulders, pin them to ground. All time I keep my grip on his throat. Now I see look of fright in his face. He proper terrified. He kick his legs, jump his body up, try throw me off. He strong man, he nearly throw me off, but I keep my hands round his neck and bang his head on ground same time, wear him out. His eyes bulge out. I try not look at that face. That face got more terror than I ever see before. Soon he stop struggle. I don't let my grip loose in case this another clever man trick. I keep squeeze and squeeze. Only when he don't move long time I let go. I let go, he still don't move. I watch him. He don't move. He don't breathe. That Muluru proper dead. Yes! I think, Jinggaya avenged and now she safe from that clever man.

I grab that dilly and run to stream belong them Mairkaioo. Stream bank show all foot print good, so I make sure grass still on feet and step from rock to rock too. Then I push that dilly down under water and haul big rock on top of him, keep him down. Now my Jinggaya get well again!

I go back near Muluru wurly. He still lie there dead, look like sleeping. Maybe them Mairkaioo don't know he dead until morning. I pick up my things. I think, that father belong Jinggaya, Yarrungaitj, he get Muluru put that spell on her. Maybe I got to kill that Yarrungaitj too before Jinggaya safe. Then I think, Jinggaya tell me her father don't treat her bad, maybe I don't kill her father. I follow trees at edge of camp down to wurly belong Yarrungaitj, same place I go when first see her. When I get near, I think of that look she give me when her father first call her. That look! That look cast some spell before she ever go to her aunt! Now, see how I love that woman! I get smile on face from think about this.

Further down camp, I see fires of corroboree, hear them Mairkaioo still dance and sing, still beat their possum skins. I leave that wallaby in front of wurly belong Yarrangaitj. I think, when he know Muluru dead he think maybe I kill that feller. When he see this wallaby, he know I leave this wallaby. Maybe he take this wallaby as sign I want peace between us, maybe he leave me and Jinggaya alone.

I leave that place and run back to my own mob.

I catch up with Mother Berangu on way back, we walk together. I tell her I kill dead that clever man, Muluru. She say nothing.

We get back to our camp. Jinggaya well! She gather plenty woman tucker, play with Monanggu and Nawngnaw. I tell her I sink that clever man dilly in water. She say she get better from that moment. I tell her I kill that clever man dead. She

152

quiet. I think, why Berangu not say she glad I kill that clever man? Why Jinggaya not say she glad I kill that clever man?

I go hunt with Cabba and Borrudum. This good, us three brothers out hunt together. We have good time, catch kangaroo and plenty small animal bring back to camp. When we back we have good feast.

Jinggaya say to me that night, 'Gunmyimbook, I talk to Mother Berangu today."

Sometimes she got a special way say my name. The way she say him this time, I know she try tell me something hard say. I know him about kill that clever man. Not sure I want hear this. I say nothing. I don't look her way.

She touch my arm and speak soft. 'Gunmyimbook … I think your Mother Berangu sad you kill that Muluru."

I angry. I say in angry voice, "Why? She tell me about Muluru. She tell me he try kill you. She tell me where find his wurly. I don't kill that Muluru, he kill you."

Jinggaya quiet long time. Then she speak in voice try make me less angry. "Yes, Gunmyimbook, all that true. She know why you kill that Muluru. But that Muluru, he her nephew, he part of her family. She still sad he die."

In the darkness I sign I understand this. I say nothing. Jinggaya go on, 'She sad you got to kill that Muluru. She say when one man kill other man

153

dead, other killing got to follow."

"Oh, yes." I still angry. "Easy for her say that. I don't kill that Muluru, he kill you dead. She got to remember that. You got to remember that."

"Yes, Gunmyimbook," she say in that voice tell me don't get angry. "That true, I know that. Berangu know that too. But you not sad you got to kill that feller?"

"That feller not harmless feller. He know how kill me, he know trick for kill me. I don't kill him, he kill me. I don't kill him, he kill you too by and by. How I sad kill that feller?"

I sense even in darkness Jinggaya got trouble. "Well, Gunmyimbook," she say, "I know you got to kill that feller, save me and save you too. I know that all true. I know the law say him right you kill that feller when he try kill you or try kill your wife or try kill your family. But still don't you think him wrong you kill that feller?"

I stare at her in darkness. I proper angry. I know I go say hurtful thing, but can't help that. "Which worse crime then? Kill feller who try kill your wife, or run away with your son-in-law?"

I hear her quiet long time. Then she start cry . She know kill that feller only crime one man against one man, but run off with son-in-law crime against whole mob, crime against ancestor and Dreaming, him much worse. When I hear her cry, I sorry I remind her about her bad crime. Me, I get punish for my crime run off with mother-in-law, I pay with spear in thigh and go through ordeal. Now I free of that crime. Jinggaya still got some of that guilt with her. She get punish by bone in heart, she get punish by sickness in head, but she don't save herself from these, she saved by other feller.

Though I hear her cry, I too angry give her any comfort. I hear her lie back and curl up, cry quiet. I don't touch her. I think, why she angry with me? Now I angry with her. She don't deserve comfort.

Later, I think this first time we proper angry with each other. I think, don't want be like Daingumbo and Dilboong, argue all time. I lie down at her back, bring my knees up warm her backside, put my arm round her, give her comfort stroke. I hear her sleep. I sleep too.

In morning, we don't say much. I still a bit angry. Jinggaya still a bit unhappy. We each got our own trouble. I think, we proper happy before, don't want be unhappy now. I think, maybe Daingumbo and Dilboong got better way, hit with stick then forget. I leave Jinggaya look after children, I go out in bush toward place where stones sit in circle. Maybe I go there, talk to Goanna, he help.

I near that place when I hear squawk come up through bush. Them squawks come nearer. I look up, see plenty white cockatoo in top of gum trees. They jump up, fly round, make plenty big noise. I know what they say. They say, "This land our land, get out."

Them cockatoo live in mobs like men. Each of their

mobs got their own bit of land same like men. When man walk in cockatoo land, them cockatoo fly off further up their land. They fly on and on as man walk more into their land. After a bit them cockatoo come to the edge of their land. They come to land belong another mob of cockatoo. That other mob, they fly up and squawk, 'This our land, get out, get out." That first mob, they squawk, 'Help! We run out of land, we got to go back. Now we got to fly near man. We don't want fly near man. Help!"

I walk off track and hide behind tree. I know some man drive them cockatoo toward me. Some man come up through bush.

I wait. Them cockatoo fly off, take their noise with them. Sound of cicada come out of trees. They all sing together, then all go quiet together. All sing together, all quiet together. After a bit, when cicadas go quiet, I hear crash come up through bush. That the crash of man running. I listen more. Two men running. I get deeper into bush, watch track.

Them two men run up. Them two men Yawingaba and Moyana! When they near, they both look my way. They don't see me, but they know I there, too right. Maybe they smell me, maybe some spirit tell them when man hide in trees. I show myself, and they stop. They pant plenty, they run long time.

I see they don't smile. They look troubled. "What go on?"

Moyana pant so much he can't speak. Yawingaba

tell me what go on. "We go to south again, watch our land for that man-beast." He stop for breath.

"You see him?" I ask.

He sign yes. "More. We see three of them man-beasts. They walk up the creek into our land. More." He pant all time. "They got men with them. Them men walk along beside them man-beast." He look more troubled. "Some of them men got no bodies!"

I sign this proper strange news. "They come this way?" I ask.

Yawingaba say, "No other way I know of. They come this way, too right."

"How long away?" I ask.

"They walk slow," say Moyana. "Like mob on move. They three day away, maybe more."

We all run back to camp, tell this to Cabba's dad and other men of our mob. Cabba's dad say this bad news. He say we got to put men back on that trail from south, warn us when man-beast come. He say men got to get their weapons and hide in bush. Women and children got to go north, hide in bush further up country.

Yawingaba and Moyana go back down trail, look out for man-beasts. I go with other men from our mob, run out into plains find our women and children who gather tucker out there. They long way out, for they clear all the tucker near camp. When we find them women and children and bring them back, that day nearly all gone. Cabba's dad say we got to keep our fires lit through the night. He say if that man-beast good spirit he don't walk at night. If he bad spirit, walk at night, he don't come near fire. We glad Cabba's dad say this. We don't like sleep without fire. We sleep without fire, all them *mamu* come get us. Don't know which I more scared of, them man-beasts or them *mamu*.

All next day we don't hear from Yawingaba and Moyana. All day after we don't hear from Yawingaba and Moyana. We think, maybe them man-beast turn back, maybe they don't come into our land. We got signs in our land, say this land belong our mob. Other mob know these signs, keep out. Maybe them man-beasts see them signs, keep out.

Then Yawingaba run into camp. He say, 'Man-beasts come. They come up creek. We watch them all time. They sleep at night, same like us. They make fire at night, same like us. They one day walk away. I leave Moyana watch them. They come tomorrow.

Them man-beasts come when Sun Woman at highest. Us men hide in trees with all our weapons. We see them man-beasts come right into our camp, walk right through him. Them man-beasts got head like kangaroo with ears point up and twist round, but they stand on four legs. They got hairy tail that flick

158

all time. They snort and breathe fire. A man come out of the middle of each beast. I proper scared. I think other men of our mob proper scared too.

Three man-beast walk into our camp. Beside them walk three men with no bodies. I see why our feller say they got no bodies. No one can see their bodies. They all covered over with stuff. They got no bodies, they got no feet, they got something cover up top of head. But then I see they got faces and they got beards all over them faces and their faces look like faces of men like us. And then I see they got hands too and their hands look like hands of men like us. In their hands they hold sticks, and I think, they got no other weapons, they only got sticks. They got no weapons for throw or cut, maybe they not so scary. We can spear them before they use their sticks, we can throw our throwing-sticks and break their legs. Then I remember them Googerak and I proper scared again.

This mob got one other feller with them, and he a man like us, except in his waist string he wear some paperbark apron like girls of some mobs wear before they made into women. He carry two spears, a waddy, a throwing stick and shield. That shield not like shield of any mob I know. He got his beard singed short. He stand in front of them others like leader. He look out at trees and we see he see us, but them men with no bodies, they look like they don't see us and I think, maybe they got no eyes.

The apron man say something to all them others. I don't know what he say, but he sound like he tell them what do. I think, this apron man, he powerful

159

feller, he tell man-beast and men with no bodies what they got to do. Then three men with no bodies step out of them beasts. Now we see three men with no bodies and three more. Them three beasts, they hold onto three of them men with no bodies, they keep them tied close with string they hold in their teeth. They got big teeth, teeth as big as a man's thumbs, they got teeth could eat up a man in two bites. Them beasts so big they could swallow a man whole.

One of them beasts say something to all them men with no bodies and shake his head at same time. I don't know what he say, but he speak very loud and I think maybe that beast the leader of that mob. I look at that beast and I see he got huge eyes as big as a man's fist and I see that them eyes see into the trees and see us watching. Then I know that beast tell the men with no bodies he see us watching.

One of them men with no bodies put his hand in the belly of a beast and pull something out. He pull out the liver of that beast. He lift the liver of that beast to his lips and drink the blood from him. Then he pass to other man with no body and that man drink the blood from him too. All them men with no bodies drink that blood from the liver of that beast. I think, this how them men with no bodies get strength of that beast. The apron man, he don't drink that blood. Then one of them men with no bodies put that liver back in the belly of the beast. One of them men with no bodies lift up the cover of his head and push his hand through his hair. I see he got hair like us and top of head like us. Then he put the cover back on.

Another one of them beasts say something proper loud. I think he tell apron man what he got to do, for next thing happen that apron man step out further in front of that mob. He walk a few paces toward the trees where we hide. Then he stop. He plant his spears and hold up clenched fist like hold fire stick. We look at one another and sign, this man want talk with us. We look towards Cabba's dad. Any man our mob talk with this mob, got to be Cabba's dad first. Cabba's dad sign us wait.

Them feller in our camp don't move. One of them beasts say something loud again. Apron man sign he come in peace, want talk. We stay behind trees. Then apron man give order to one of them men with no bodies. That man with no body go to beast and pull out axe from belly of beast. That beast got axe for rib. Man with no body show us axe. He got grey stone head gleam in light, he look proper sharp. Man with no body get thick branch of tree, lay on other branch nearby. Then he chop that axe on that branch. He chop through that branch in three chops. Now we know that proper good axe. Best axe in our mob that axe belong Cabba's dad. He take five chops and five chops more get through that branch.

I think, they show that axe make us scared. I think, they chop them Googerak babies in two with that axe. They chop off them heads and them arms of them Googerak with that axe. Now they show us that axe make us scared. He make me scared, that sure.

Man with no body hold up axe by head with shaft

towards us. Same time that apron man say something to us. He got strange lingo. I don't understand all of him but I think he say this axe a gift for our mob. Then he speak in signs. These signs I understand good. These signs say he come in peace, he give axe as gift.

I think, these men with no bodies carry only stick for weapon. That axe their best weapon. That axe only good weapon they got. That apron man, he got good weapons, but them men with no bodies they only got sticks and that axe. I don't see more axes. I think, why they want give us their best weapon? I think, maybe they know we don't use that weapon, maybe they know we don't fight with axe, against our law. I think again, maybe they think we don't know they use this axe like weapon, maybe they don't know I see what they do to Googerak. I think, I see their trick. They offer us gift of axe, our leader come out for get him, then they turn axe and chop our leader in pieces like I see with them Googerak.

I turn to Cabba's dad and sign him this gift a trick. I sign him, remember what I see in Nose-Bone country. I sign him, remember I see plenty feller in that country chopped to pieces by men with no bodies. Cabba's dad sign he understand. We all keep behind trees.

All them feller keep still for a bit. Then one of them beasts speak loud again, give order to apron man. Apron man walk back, take axe from man with no body. He bring that axe towards trees, put him on ground. Then he walk backwards away from axe. He leave that axe same distance from our mob as from their mob.

Cabba's dad sign me, what trick here?

I sign, I don't know.

Cabba's dad don't go for axe. We all keep behind trees, watch what happen. That other mob all stand look at trees, watch axe. I remember what Mother Berangu say about patient feller. Cabba's dad sign all our mob keep behind trees.

One of them beasts drop shit. His shit huge, drop to ground with splat, make big pile. His shit big as that shit of that beast with two heads we see east of lake in north. I look at Cabba's dad, sign him, why that beast drop shit where we can see him?

Cabba's dad sign he don't know. He sign, we make spell on that shit when beast go, kill that beast dead if we want to. Maybe that beast don't know how strong our magic. We still keep behind trees, wait, watch what happen.

After a bit that other mob get tired wait for us make move. We see them talk to each other. Then one of them climb back into one of them beast so that beast man-beast again. Man-beast turn away and run off into our valley. He run faster than emu. He so big we feel the ground shake under his feet. As he run off, I see them feet underneath like twig bent for hoop. Now I sure these same man-beast that kill all them Googerak.

That man-beast go out of sight and we don't hear his noise. Everything go quiet. The mob left behind don't move much. Some of them sit or squat. Sun Woman start to climb down towards hills in north west. Then from the valley we hear one big shout. We see that mob left behind stand up, talk to each other.

After a bit we feel the ground shake and hear the noise of that man-beast. His feet bang on the ground like feller beat possum-skin rug across knees at corroboree. Then that man-beast run back into camp and stop. We hear the breath of that man-beast. That man-beast breathe louder than any man or beast. He breathe loud from run hard. We see that man step out of that beast again. Then he reach into belly of beast and pull out big kangaroo! He hold this kangaroo up, show him to all the feller in that mob.

I close my eyes. I think, do I really see this? This not possible. Do I really hide behind this tree, or do I sleep and dream all this? I open my eyes and look across at Cabba's dad. I see look in his face that say he don't believe what he see. I think I got that same look. I believe what I see, then that man-beast run out into valley, catch kangaroo, swallow him whole in one gulp, bring him back and deliver him to that mob. He do all this in less time than Sun Woman take for climb down sky from her highest place half way to hills.

We see all them men with no bodies gather round kangaroo. Then one of them call apron man come pick up kangaroo. He pick up that kangaroo over shoulder, carry him towards us hidden in trees. He put that kangaroo down next to that axe that still lie in the grass.

We all look at that kangaroo. He big kangaroo, he make plenty good feast for lucky feller who cook him. We look at that axe. He proper sharp axe, cut through branch proper quick.

We look at that kangaroo. No trick in that kangaroo. Any man pick up that kangaroo, he got good animal, proper good tucker. We look at that axe. Maybe no trick in that axe, like no trick in that kangaroo. Any man pick up that axe got proper sharp axe, cut through branch proper quick.

We look at them men with no bodies. They got no weapons apart from their sticks. We look at them beasts. They don't make noise like they going to attack. We look at that apron man. He got his spears planted, he stand back, sign for us to take tucker, take axe.

Cabba's dad sign us keep behind trees, keep our spears ready. Then he step out from trees and walk up to that kangaroo and that axe.

Cabba's dad stop near that kangaroo and that axe. He don't pick them up. He keep look at that other mob. That other mob don't move. Apron man sign Cabba's dad take kangaroo and axe for gift.

Some of us men step out of trees and walk up behind Cabba's dad. We got our spears ready in

165

our spear-throwers.

Cabba's dad sign that apron man. He sign, this camp our camp, this land our land, this kangaroo our kangaroo.

Apron man sign he come like friend. He sign, take axe, take kangaroo.

I see Cabba's dad look good at that axe. I see he think that axe proper good gift, maybe he let these feller stay a bit. He turn to me and say, "Bradek, run to my wurly. Inside I got good possum skin rug and coolamon. Bring rug and coolamon here quick."

I run to wurly, come back quick, give those things to Cabba's dad. Cabba's dad put those things on ground behind kangaroo and axe, towards that other mob. He say to apron man, "This good possum skin rug. This good coolamon. You take as gift."

Apron man understand these words. He sign yes. He step forward and pick up them things. Then he say in strange lingo, "Your women sew good possum skin rug. Good as any mob make. Your men carve good coolamon. Good as any mob carve." His lingo like lingo belong mobs south of us, but not same. Like some of one, some of other, some we don't know. But Cabba's dad like his words.

Cabba's dad step forward and pick up axe. He feel edge of that axe blade. He say, "Your men make good axe, proper sharp. Your men catch kangaroo bloody quick."

Apron man and Cabba's dad stand close. Cabba's dad say, "Where you make your journey?"

Apron man point down creek. "We come from south." He point to our plains. "We go over them plains. Then we go back south."

Cabba's dad say, "Them plains our plains. We don't let strange mob go on our plains."

Apron man look troubled at this. He look back at them men and beasts in his mob. "All these feller want go to them plains."

Cabba's dad say, "You their leader, you tell them can't go on our plains. You got to go back way you come."

Apron man turn to men with no bodies and say something in lingo we don't know. We see them laugh a bit, then speak back at apron man.

Cabba's dad say, "Why they laugh?"

Apron man say, "They laugh when you think I their leader."

Cabba's dad quiet for a bit. Then he say, "Who your leader then? Is he this beast?" He point to beast nearest, one who speak loud before.

Apron man speak again to men with no bodies. They laugh a lot. Then apron man say to Cabba's dad, "No, these beast take order from these feller." He speak again to men with no bodies. One of those men walk up to beast who hold him by string, push that beast on the neck. That beast turn round when man push him. Then man with no body push that beast back and we see that beast walk backwards when man push. Then that man pull string forward and we see beast walk forward. Now we see that man with no body give order to beast.

"What kind of beast is that?" ask Cabba's dad. "He big as four men but he take orders from one man. What kind of beast?"

Apron man say, "He 'horse.'"

"What that horse eat?"

"Horse eat grass. He don't eat any other tucker." We all look surprised.

"Why he got such big teeth when he only eat grass?"

Apron man sign he don't know.

"Where them horse come from?" ask Cabba's dad.

"These feller bring them horse here in big canoe from land across waters."

I know when our feller die their spirit go to island across big waters. I think, them feller come from that place. They got to be ghosts. Cabba's dad think same. He say, "Them men with no bodies, they ghost then?"

Apron man laugh. "No, they not ghost. They men."

"Why they got no bodies then?"

Apron man turn and speak to men with no bodies. They all laugh a lot. I don't like their laugh. We don't laugh with them. Then one of them men with no bodies say something to other man with no body. We see number one man point, number two man sign no. Then number two man sit on ground and number one man get hold of one of his feet and try pull him off. After a bit, that foot come off, and we see inside that foot that man got another foot with toes like foot of man. That foot all white.

Then number one man pull on other foot, and that come off too, and we see that feller sit on ground got two feet with toes like feet of man. Both them feet all white. His brown feet without toes stand on ground beside him.

Then that man stand up and take off his head cover and we see he got hair like man. He bend forward a bit and pull off his own skin over his head. He pull that skin off from the waist up. He pull that skin off and drop him on ground, and we see under that skin he got another skin with shoulders and chest like shoulders and chest of man. That skin all white.

He stand there and look at us. The number one man with no body say something to him. Then we see him peel off his skin from the waist down. He peel off that skin, pull him over his feet and drop him on the ground. We see that man got white legs, legs like legs of man but white. We see that man white all over, white like ghost, except for his face and hands, which brown like face and hands of man.

Cabba's dad say, 'This man a ghost! Why he got no cock if he man?"

Apron man say, 'He not ghost! He man same like you but white skin." Then he say something to number one man with no body and all them feller in that mob laugh a lot, some of them fall on ground or bend over laugh so much. When stop laughing, that number one man with no body say something to ghost man and ghost man sign no. Then number one man speak again to ghost man, and ghost man peel off another layer of skin from the waist down. He peel off that skin over his legs and pull him off over his feet and drop him on ground. Now we see that man got a cock like a man and he got black hairs all over his white legs.

Cabba's dad say to apron man, 'This man full grown, but he still got foreskin on his cock! Why he not made into man?"

Apron man answer, 'White feller don't cut off that foreskin like black feller. But he full grown man all right."

Cabba's dad say, 'Who this black feller you talk of?"

Apron man say, 'You, me, all them feller behind you. They black fellers. That what white feller call us mobs."

Cabba's dad say, 'But we brown colour like brown snake or gum nut, not black like crow. Why they call us black feller?"

Apron man sign he don't know. "That's what they call us," he say.

Cabba's dad say, "Why you cover your cock with apron, like girl nearly woman?"

Apron man sign he troubled at this. "Them white feller, they tell me I got to do this," he say.

Cabba's dad quiet for a bit. "You not the leader of this mob then? Who leader of your mob then?"

Apron man look troubled again. "These feller not my mob. My mob over there." He point far away to south. "These white feller don't speak our lingo. They catch me long time back, teach me their lingo. They take me to their wurlies, give me their drink and their food. Some proper good tucker. They don't give me any woman though. They give me plenty meat. I eat these beasts, these horse, and other beasts them white feller bring. Them beasts proper good tucker. They give me plenty fish. They give me sweet brown drink they call tea, he taste like that sweet water our women make when find good nectar, but they make that tea all time and make him hot. They give me all these things but they make sure I don't run away. I learn their lingo good. Then they take me with them for guide when go in strange country. They take me all time. I don't see my wife or my children or anyone of my old mob long time."

"Why don't you run away?" ask Cabba's dad. "Why don't you run away now, get back to your mob?"

Apron man sign this hard. "You don't know power of these white feller," he say. "You see. I try run away plenty in old days, they catch me every time. Now I know I can't run away."

That ghost man, he cover up his white body again while apron man talk with Cabba's dad. Then the number one man with no body, the number one white feller, call out to apron man and tell him something.

Apron man say to Cabba's dad, "That feller who speak, he the leader of this mob. He called Mallee. He ask what you called."

Cabba's dad don't answer for a bit. I know he think same as me: he give that white feller his name, maybe that white feller put spell on him. Cabba's dad say, "Tell him my name Turnung." We all know Turnung not name belong Cabba's dad and we know why he don't say his name. Then Cabba's dad say, "Ask your leader Mallee why he come to our land."

Apron man talk with Mallee. Mallee come closer to Cabba's dad. Apron man say, "Mallee ask if these plains got water." He point to plains down our valley.

Cabba's dad say, "Tell him, he thirsty, he can drink in our stream. We got water in our stream."

Apron man say, "He not thirsty. He ask if plenty water down there, in plains."

Cabba's dad say, "Sometimes plenty water in plains, sometimes none. When rain, plenty water. When dry, none. Dry season come now. Our stream dry up, all them plains proper dry. Kangaroo and wallaby go away look for water. We burn that dry grass under trees on plain. When wet season come back, grass come with new shoot, proper green and good. Them kangaroo and wallaby come back, eat good grass. Why Mallee want know this?"

Apron man talk with Mallee and then say, "Mallee say we go down to plains now. He say he give good knife sharp like axe to black feller who come with us, show us where water run in that plain."

Cabba's dad send Cabba show white feller where water run. After they go, Cabba's dad tell all us men follow them white feller, hide in trees, make sure they don't try catch Cabba like they catch apron man. We follow, they don't see us. Apron man see us, but them white feller don't see us. We follow two days. Then white feller go off and Cabba come back to us.

"Where white feller go?" we ask.

"They go off, back to their own country. I show them where water run, they go off, leave me come back alone."

"They don't go off way they come," we say. "They know this country?"

"No," say Cabba. "They got strong magic. They got magic bone, they let him swing, he always point way back to their camp." Then he look excited. "See

173

this knife!" He show us knife. He made from same grey stone like axe, but he big knife. He got long blade but that blade proper thin. That thin blade, he don't break easy like thin stone, he strong. That knife good knife, stay sharp long time.

When we back at camp, Cabba's dad call us all together. "Now we go find our women, bring them back," he say. "Then time we go to lake in north."

When we come back to that camp near Goanna Rock, plenty rain fall and all that grass in valley good and green. Monanggu and Nawngnaw grow big, walk and run good. Monnangu talk good, she care for her brother all time, she care like mother. Nawngnaw got no fear, he go anywhere fearless, I glad Monanngu look out for him. They play with other children all day in our stream which full of water.

Our feller go out on plains for catch kangaroo. I go with Moyana and Yawingaba to Goanna Rock, paint up that sign good. Moyana make new song for Goanna. We learn this song and sing him at that Goanna Rock. Song go:

Goanna tongue flick out round rock.
Goanna tongue flick out,
Keep all us mob safe from white feller.

We make dance go with this song. We all got to walk like goanna in that dance. We sing that song, do that dance long time. We feel good, sing that song, do that dance. I happy man. Sun Woman come over Goanna Rock, warm us up good when we sing and dance. I think, I happy man. I got beautiful woman wait at my fire, work hard gather tucker, make dilly, gather firewood. I got happy children play in stream. Monanggu got happy nature like her own mother, she already got that little laugh like her own mother got. She play with baby I carve from wood. She make good mother when she woman. Nawngnaw don't say much, but he make fine man when grow up. He play with toy spear all time, he make good hunter when he man.

Our feller come back from hunt. They catch one kangaroo. They say not many kangaroo down on plains. They say that grass in plains all eaten short, but not by kangaroo. They say some other beast eat that grass, leave shit on ground not like kangaroo shit. They say beast that eat that grass got small feet with no toes. Cabba's dad say this some magic of them white feller, we got to all go and find out what happen down there.

We paint up big war party in case them white feller down in plains and make trouble. We take all our weapons and run into plain as big party. We see that short grass and that strange shit. We see where them beast with no toes walk. Cabba's dad say, 'This not like beast with no toes we see east of lake in north. This much smaller beast. But they many, many like ants."

We go three days into our country, follow river that run through that land after rain. We follow that river, we find him widen out into flooded land. We never see flood in that part before. That flooded land full of trees. We see them trees got leaf fall, dead branch. Them trees start die for be too wet. This flood got to be here long time make trees die. We wade through that flood, he get deep in parts nearly to waist.

We wade to edge of flooded land. We hear that strange beast first time. He call out with cry like crow, ka-a-a-a, but more quick. Then through trees we see beasts near edge of flood, where trees thin and grass grow. Them beast run away when they see us come, with cry of ka-a-a-a. We run after them. They many beast, many like ants. They swarm all over that grass, run away from us with loud cries, ka-a-a-a, ka-a-a-a. But they don't run fast, don't run far. We run after them. They get blocked by rocky land, they scatter both sides. Cabba's dad run in and throw his spear, get one of them beast in body. We throw more spears into that beast. He got plenty spear in him, he fall down on ground. Them other beast run off. We all run up close and gather round that beast, take a good look at him.

He got head and ears like kangaroo, but he stand on four legs. His feet got no toes. His body covered in long fur. That fur rough, not smooth like roo fur or possum fur. Cabba's dad say, 'We kill this hairy beast! Now we eat him! Make a fire!"

We make a big fire for cook that beast. We cut him open. He got guts like roo guts. We cut off them feet and pull out his sinews. His sinews not long like roo sinews, they don't bind much axe. Then we feel ground shake and noise of feet stamp earth. We know that sound! Him that sound of man-beast we hear before. We look about, see man-beast come over ridge. He stop when he see us. We see that horse stand up on back legs like kangaroo, then on all four legs again. That white feller shake his stick at us. We shake our spears at him, shout, "Go away, ghost man! Get off our land!" Cabba's dad tell us spread out, keep our spear ready. When that white feller see how many warrior we got, he scared, he order that horse run away. He run off back over the ridge and we hear the sound of them horse feet run away, get more quiet and more quiet again until hear no more.

Cabba's dad say, "Let us skin this beast while that fire burn down to ashes! Let us see what his skin like!" So we skin that beast and he skin good, he skin like kangaroo. We scrape his skin and we see when that skin dry he make good skin for sleep on when night cold.

When that fire burn down to ashes, Sun Woman go down behind hills, start her journey through hole in earth back to east for morning. We make camp fires and wurlies, cook that beast in them ashes. We don't cook him long, for we proper hungry! We eat that beast and he taste good, he got good grease and good meat. His kidneys and his heart and his brains and his liver all good, we all taste a little bit of them parts. He got plenty meat, too. We all excited eat this new beast, talk about him long time by camp fire, sing song and dance. Cabba's dad make up song about this beast. He go,

White feller beast got no toes.
White feller run away, leave his beast!
Plenty meat on that beast for all our warrior!

Cabba's dad sing this song. Other feller learn him, keep him going. We clap our hands to sound of words. More feller sing him, other feller stamp feet in dance. We sing, clap, stamp. When some feller get tired, other feller take over. We keep that song and that dance going long time. I happy be with my mob that night.

In the morning when Sun Woman only gleam through trees, we feel that ground shake again, and hear the feet of them man-beasts stamp the earth. This time we hear many feet. We spread out with our spears ready in case they attack us. We hear them feet stamp nearer and louder. Then four man-beast come on top of ridge. They stop there and look down at us. We look back at them, spears ready.

One of them men get down from that beast, that horse, and walk towards us. He take off his head cover as he walk towards us, and we see he that same feller talk to us before, that apron man who man like us. This time he come on horse! This time he got his body covered over like white feller! He walk down the slope towards us. We see he still got feet same like us. He only got stick for weapon. He hold up his fist, show he come in peace, and he stop about a spear throw away. He call out, 'Turnung! I got to speak with you."

Cabba's dad walk toward that apron man. "Apron

man!" he call out. "Why you cover yourself like white feller?"

Apron man lean on his stick. "They say I got to. They give me all these things for cover my body. These things too hot! These things no good! But they say I got to be same like them. They teach me sit on horse, give that horse orders. Now I know how give that horse orders, he take me anywhere. Them white feller, they feed me, they give me plenty sweet drink and tucker for look after their beasts they call sheep. Now I look after their sheep good."

Cabba's dad say, "You can come in our mob. We take you like brother, you can throw away all them covers. Come now, run to us, we save you from them white feller."

Apron man look over his shoulder at them three man-beast still on the ridge. He look like he think about run to us like Cabba's dad say. Then he sign no. "You don't know the power of these white feller," he say. "I run to you, they kill me dead damn quick. Right now, they proper angry. They angry you kill one of their sheep."

Cabba's dad say, "This sheep on our land. Any beast on our land our beast. This sheep drink our water. All this our water. Any beast drink our water our beast."

Apron man look troubled. "This water not your water," he say. "This water gathered by white feller. Them white feller block your river with

179

stones further down." He point through floods. "Them stones stop this water flow down river. This water, he gather here, flood all this land."

"This water our water," say Cabba's dad. We see he got anger in his face and anger in his voice, but he try keep that anger inside him, not let him out. We got anger inside us too. We see Cabba's dad keep him in, so we keep him in too. "This water made from rain that fall on our land. All this plain, all this water, belong our mob. This our land all over as far as Mairkaioo country. We don't want white feller on our land. We don't want white feller block our river with stones. Tell him he got to go now!"

We call out from behind Cabba's dad, "Yes! Tell white feller he got to go now!" We shake our spears, let some anger out.

Apron man look more troubled. He walk slow back to them man-beast on top of ridge, talk to them a bit. Then he walk back slow again. When he speak he got troubled voice.

"These white feller say this plain with all this grass and all these floods belong their mob. They say your mob keep that land over toward your camp, up that valley. White feller say they need this land for feed their sheep on the grass."

Cabba's dad beat his chest, speak in angry voice. "This grass belong our mob. This grass feed our kangaroo and our wallaby. Too little grass for feed white feller sheep as well. White feller got to go back, take his sheep back where come from."

Apron man say, 'They don't do that. They say your mob got to keep up that valley where you got your camp. They say, you catch their sheep, they catch you and kill you dead. They say you got to go back to your camp now.'

Cabba's dad shake his spear and shout out in proper angry voice, 'This land our land! Let the flesh of the white feller fall from his body, let the blow-fly blow on his flesh!'

All us mob shout, 'Yes! Yes! We eat the fat round the kidneys of the white feller! Let the curse of Turnung kill them all dead!' We shake our spears and roar out our curses.

We see apron man proper troubled at curse from Cabba's dad. That proper bad curse. Apron man turn and run back up the hill to them white feller.

Cabba's dad say, 'My Giant Yam say he rise up and crush them white feller!'

Cabba say, 'My Brown Snake bite them white feller and kill them dead with his poison!'

Borrudum say, 'My Honey Ant trample them white feller!'

I say, 'My Goanna run up over them white feller!'

Cabba's dad say, 'Them man-beast proper big, but they only got stick for weapon. We go after them now, kill dead all them feller who try take our land! We eat the fat round the kidneys of our enemy!"

We all shout, "We eat the fat round the kidneys of our enemy!" and we run up that hill after them man-beast. We see Apron Man climb up on his beast and order him run off quick. Them white feller shout after him, but he don't stop. We hear his horse run off behind the ridge.

Them white feller stay on top of that ridge. We spread out into trees and work up to ridge both sides of them white feller.

We nearly up to them on ridge, we nearly close enough throw spear when I see one of them white feller point his stick at our mob on other side, look along his stick and shout loud. He shout so loud we all surprised. Then all of them man-beast run off behind the ridge and we hear the feet of their horses beat on the ground more and more quiet. We run up on to top of ridge. We don't see them white feller, we don't hear their horses. We shout, "We eat the fat round the kidneys of our enemy!" and shake our spears and shields and dance wild, for we know we frighten away them white feller. We frighten them right off our land.

We see some of our mob stay lower down. They gather round fallen warrior. We run down to them, find out what happen. That fallen man, he one of my uncles. "What happen? What happen?" we all ask.

We see that fallen warrior got wound in belly. He

got trouble breathing. He say, 'That white feller, he point his stick at me. I see him look down him, look right at me, then shout. Then I get this pain in belly."

Cabba's dad got his finger in hole in belly belong that fallen warrior. He say, 'This feller got a stone in his belly. The white feller shout that stone into his belly! That white feller got evil eye, he look with evil eye on our warrior, he shout this stone into his belly."

That fallen warrior proper crook. Cabba's dad proper clever man, he cut that man's belly and pull out his guts. Then we give that feller a drink for show any leak in his guts. He got leak all right. Cabba's dad say, 'This feller proper crook, he die soon." He sew up that leak and pack them guts back into that feller with grass and clay, but that feller don't look too good. By and by he die. His brothers hit their heads with stones, make blood cover their faces and run down bodies show their grief. We all sad this feller die. Cabba's dad say too far carry him back to camp, we got to leave his body here. So we make tree platform for his body and cover him with logs and branches, keep off them eagles until the flesh fall from his body and we can bury him, rest his spirit good.

Sun Woman go down so we make camp under that ridge. In the morning we follow the tracks of them man-beast and all them sheep. They go round beside that water and off to south, but so many tracks of them sheep and them horses we not sure which way they go day before. Then we come to end of flood and see them stones those white feller put to stop up that river. Plenty of them stones, stop up that river good. We think, more stones here than four men can put. Plenty of them stones, they stop up that river wider than a spear throw.

We go careful down to stones in case they got some kind of trick, but we don't see any trick. Then Cabba's dad say, "Pull these stones down!" We all go out on them stones, pull them out, put branch in push them out. We take out all them stones in middle of the river, and that water he rush out where we take out stones and he push more stones out of the way. Soon that river flow good again, and we all dance and clap see that river flow again.

When that river flow again, we all go back to our camp near Goanna Rock. Wife of that fallen warrior, she proper sad he die, she beat her head with stone till blood run, she cry out, she mourn him. I think, I don't want die, I don't want Jinggaya mourn me.

I go with Grandfather Moyana and Uncle Yawingaba up to Goanna Rock. We feel good, look out from that rock, see all that bush and valley and plain, know those white feller run away leave us our land. Down in camp, Jinggaya come back from gather woman tucker, we family again round our fireplace. I play with Monanggu and Nawngnaw, tell them some of our stories from Dreamtime. At night we sleep in our wurly all together. I hold Jinggaya. Monanggu and Nawngnaw hold each other, sleep at our heads.

Many days pass. Then Borrudum come back from hunt, say he see man-beast again near that flood land where water now drained. He say many of them man-beast make camp in that land. He touch top of head for number of them man-beast; he mean he count five for fingers on hand, five for points from wrist to shoulder, five for points from neck to top of head. He leave other Honey Ant out in that place, keep watch on them man-beast.

The next day them other Honey Ant run into camp, say the man-beast walk this way one day travel. Cabba's dad tell all us men get ready for big fight. He say all our warrior go down valley, meet them man-beast with our spears and clubs. He say we got to not look at them white feller, not look in their faces, so they don't look at us with evil eye. Cabba's dad say our young women got to fight too. They got to make line behind us men. Cabba's dad say all our children got to stay in camp with old women, ready to run into bush in case them man-beast get past us.

We make more fighting spear, get them straight by heat over fire, sharpen them spear points good by rub on rock. Every man check his spear sharp.

Cabba's dad say them man-beast only fight with sticks and evil eye. He say we don't look at their faces. We don't look at their faces, they can't kill us with evil eye. He say we kill them easy with our spears and clubs. He say, remember how they run away when they see how many warrior we got. All our warrior shout "We eat the fat round the kidneys of our enemy!" They shake their spear and say

185

what they do to white feller. They all dance round fire, stamp ground, beat shields and chest, get fired up. I join in, but my *yowi* speak to me: he say, Bradek, you pretend. You not really fired up. You got trouble. You got doubts. You see what them man-beast do to them Googerak. These other feller don't see what them man-beast do to Googerak.

Mother Berangu look after Monanggu and Nawng-naw. I say to her, "Mother, I get killed in this battle, Jinggaya get killed in this battle, take these children to Nose-Bone country. Them Nose Bones know these children, they look after them. Tell them they children of Nantoomana, brother of Daingumbo."

Jinggaya paint herself up with white clay like warrior. I say to her, "Jinggaya, I get killed in this battle, run to Nose-Bone country. You safe with Daingumbo and Dilboong, they look after you all."

Jinggaya touch my arm and she give that little laugh I love. That laugh not so happy like normal, I see in her face she got trouble too, but I still love that laugh. "Bradek," she say in quiet voice, "remember, Nantoomana don't get killed in battle."

I touch her hand. I say to her, "You good woman, Jinggaya. You best wife feller ever have." I like say more, but words don't come. Then I put that bone in my nose. Jinggaya laugh, like first time. I laugh too. But I glad know I Nantoomana, I don't get killed in battle. Then we join with other warrior and walk out down valley.

Us warrior make a big line down that valley, our women warrior behind us. This a big crowd of warrior. We feel good, proper strong. We know no enemy beat this big crowd of warrior. We chant, "We eat the kidneys of our enemy" as we walk down valley. We stamp our feet, bang our shield with club, make big noise, scare them white feller.

We see them man-beast down in the valley. Them white feller keep on top of them horse. We see them stopped in a line across our valley. They don't run away, they wait for us walk closer.

We walk to a spear throw away. We see them horse watch us with their big eyes. I remember not look in face of white man. Our mob stop. We shout, "We eat the kidneys of our enemy!" and bang our shields with big noise. I see some of them horse walk back a bit. I think, them horse frightened! I don't look at white feller, I don't know he frightened or not.

We wait in our line. This our way do battle with other mob. Leaders call out, maybe find some way don't have big fight, plenty feller killed and killed dead. Plenty time mobs line up in battle, don't get big fight. Maybe settle one man one man, maybe find other way than fight. Big fight, plenty men killed dead both sides, no good for either mob.

Cabba's dad walk out front. He call out, "Ho! You white feller, you take our land, you take our grass, you take our water! All these things belong our mob!" He wait for leader other side make answer.

I see them white feller all lift their sticks, point them at our mob. I think, Oh no! they look evil eye on us! I close my eyes so they can't get me. I hear great shout come from them white feller. I open my eyes, I see them horse breathe fire. I see plenty warrior our mob fallen to ground. I don't understand this, how many warrior our mob fall to ground. I see Cabba's dad turn, look at his line of warrior, see all them feller fallen to ground. He run to one, then to another, then to another. I see he proper troubled. Then he call out to us, "They kill us with shout from long away! We got to run all about, run around them, run in close, kill them with our spear!"

We start run when we see them point their sticks again and give another shout. More of our warrior fall to ground. We run in, throw our spear, but them man-beast already run away down valley. We run after them. We run quick, but them horse run much faster than man. We run after them, glad see them run away. But down valley they stop again. I run in with others, ready throw my spear. Then I see them white feller point their sticks again. I hear them shout again. I see them horse breathe fire again. And I see many warrior of our mob fall to ground again. We run in throw our spear, but them man-beast run off down valley again. We run after them. They stop again. This time we know they use evil eye shout us dead so we don't run in, we run to side. They still point their sticks at us when we run to side. They shout again. Their horse breathe fire again. More of our warrior fall to ground.

I look about me. I see all that valley covered with

our warrior. I see them lie on ground or crawl or sit up. I hear them call out. Behind them our line of women still stand. They protect way to camp. Down the valley are them man-beast. I hear their horse breathe hard after run. I think, not many of our men left standing. Do them man-beast run away again? I see they don't. They run towards us! They come kill those men left standing!

"Run for trees!" I hear Cabba's dad call. I run for trees at edge of valley. I hear the feet of them horse bang on the earth as they run toward us. I look over shoulder, see them man beast run down our warrior. They don't shout this time. I see them run down our warrior with stick that gleam in sun, hit our warrior with that stick. I see our warrior fall down. Then I reach trees and I see them man-beast don't follow us into trees.

I hide behind tree panting. I think maybe two other warrior in trees my side. They hide behind tree too. I don't see them. I think maybe three warrior reach trees on other side of valley. I don't see them now. I climb up tree, get view of valley. I see all our warrior lie down or crawl in that valley. I see them white feller order their horse run up the valley to where our warrior lie or crawl. I see them hit them with them sticks. I see one of our warrior get up on knees, I see that white feller hit stick on neck, I see our warrior head fall to ground! I see other warrior get arm cut off. I see all them wounded warrior get killed dead, and I think of them Googerak. This how all them Googerak get killed dead, how they get their arms and heads cut off and how their baby get cut in two. Not with axe, but with this sharp

189

stick them white feller got. I see some of them white feller get off their horse and walk about, hit our feller lie on ground with that sharp stick. I think, Oh no! all them warrior get killed dead! All the men in our mob get killed dead!

I see our women still make line at top of valley. I see them white feller that walk get back on their horse and all them feller order their horse run up the valley towards our women. I think, Oh no! Jinggaya, don't fight these white feller, they kill you dead! You got no men left help you fight these white feller. I send this thought to her, Run Jinggaya! Run! Run to Nose-Bone country! I send this thought to Berangu, Run Berangu! Run to Nose-Bone country! I see some women break from line and start run. Them other women, they see all that happen down valley, they know they can't fight white feller. When some start run they all start run. They turn and run back towards camp or towards trees at side of valley. Them horse run fast up the valley, I see them run after our women. I see them sharp stick gleam in sun when them white feller hit our women as they run. They hit and hit. Many women fall. I think some reach trees. I see our women on ground. I see some of them white men get down from horse and walk among them women, hit them with stick same like men. I think, Oh no! all them women get killed dead! All the women in our mob get killed dead!

I think, do I run up there, try save Jinggaya? Then I think, I run up there, they kill me dead, too right. I got no hope save Jinggaya. She save herself or she don't get saved. I think, do I run out and attack

them white feller, get killed like them other warrior? But then I think, if Jinggaya live, I don't want
die. I love that woman. She need me.

I see them white feller order their horses run into
our camp. I can't see our camp. I hear many loud
shout come from that way, and I think maybe them
white feller try kill our women and children with
shout in camp. This terrible thought, but I run up
there find truth they kill me dead too right. Them
white feller in our camp long time, but I don't come
out of trees. I think, maybe they come back soon,
they see me, they kill me with shout. I hear more
shouts come from camp way. By and by I see them
man-beast come walk down from camp way. They
walk some this side of valley, some other side of
valley. They look in the trees. I see one of them
white feller raise his stick and shout into trees. I
think, now they look for us feller who hide in trees,
kill him dead with shout. Soon they come my way.
I climb down from tree quick, run off into bush.

By and by I don't hear any more shout. I wait, make
sure them white feller go away. Then I creep back
to edge of trees, take look around valley. Trees
make long shadow all over valley as Sun Woman
go down. I don't see any man-beast. I think, maybe
they hide in trees, wait for me come out. I remember how Mother Berangu teach me patience. I wait
in trees, keep good look out. Mother Berangu! How
I want know how you are. My children! Where are
you? Are you dead? Jinggaya! Woman I love more
than anything in this world, what happen to you?
Oh, this terrible wait!

When light dim I run to warrior fall near. He dead! Ai, ai! I run to other warrior. He dead. Ai, ai! I run from one warrior to another. All dead! I feel that water come to my eyes. All them warrior dead! Then I find body of Borrudum on grass. He got cut throat, blood all down chest. Borrudum dead! Borrudum my initiation brother, Borrudum I play with when child, hunt with when man. I don't see too good now, so much water come from eyes. I see more dead fellow. Then I find head of Cabba in grass. His body near. Cabba! Cabba my other brother from initiation! Cabba, how can you be dead? Cabba, I play with you too, and hunt with you too. You always good friend. How can you be dead?

I walk that valley like I no longer alive myself. Every step I take I see body of warrior. Body of Uncle Yawingaba lie near trees on other side. Yawingaba! My brother Goanna! Never go to Goanna Rock again, never help me paint that sign, never sing our Goanna song, do our dance. Yawingaba, who slit his cock at my initiation! Oh, Yawingaba, you can't be dead. Yawingaba, you always keep near Granddad Moyana. Where Moyana go, Yawingaba go too, you love that old man. Moyana got to be near this place. I look about. There! In long grass near trees. Moyana! I run up to him. Ai, ai! You dead! All you feller dead! Every man in that valley dead!

I think, I want be dead too! Goanna, why you save me but let my brothers die? Better I dead than live when all my brother dead. All my brother die in battle. I should die in battle too! Then I think, you

Nantoomana! Parangal say you never die in battle! When he say this, you think him a blessing! Now you know him a curse!

I stand up and pull that bone out of my nose, throw him to ground. I stand at head of that valley and I beat my chest and shout out down him, "Come, white feller, come kill me too! Come! I Bradek, I one of this mob! Come kill me now, like you kill my brothers!"

I hear my voice go down that valley in that night air and come back up to me. No sound of horse feet bang on ground. No shout from white feller point stick. No sound except sound of animals always in that valley. Crickets rattle and frogs sing. Kookaburra give his go sleep call. Them laughs sound out round that valley. I think, don't laugh, kookaburra, don't laugh. Time you learn how cry. I fall on my knees and show him good how a feller cry.

When I get some strength back I walk up to our camp. Moon Man don't come with his torch that time, but all that way lit up by the fires of our ancestors who got their camp in the sky. I think how many more fires there be soon when spirit of our dead feller join that camp.

I walk slow at top of valley where them white feller kill our women. I don't want look about here, don't want see all them dead women, don't want find Jinggaya in among them dead women. But I look.

How I do this I don't know. Maybe I see so many dead feller I don't feel much more pain.

I see women lie in grass. I think, don't let one of them women be Jinggaya. I walk to one woman. She not Jinggaya, she wife of one of them men feller who lie down the valley. I walk to another woman. She not Jinggaya, she wife one of them feller too. I walk woman to woman, each time I think, she not Jinggaya. I walk in daze, I don't know what think. All them women dead, dead like them Googerak, dead like them men.

Women lie in that grass all way to tree line. I find my own mother dead in that grass. Oh no! My own mother, she lie dead in that grass, her body all cut by white feller stick. I hit my head with stones, that hot blood gush out and pour down my face, but that pain from know my own mother dead more bad. Oh mother, you brave mother, you fight with young women because you got no grandchildren need you in camp. Oh mother, I fear your husband lie dead down that valley, my own father, but I don't find him.

I got no time mourn my mother proper good. I got to find Jinggaya. I think maybe women lie in long grass near trees, or crawl into bush for die. Maybe Jinggaya in there. I go to edge of trees, but too dark in there for see anything. I got to wait for Sun Woman make sure. I hurry in dark to camp.

No fire in camp. No feller in that camp. They all dead or run away. I look about, find more dead feller. I find three old women and two old men

194

dead. Maybe they never leave camp. I find some children and baby dead. Maybe they looked after by old men and women. I don't find Monanggu or Nawngnaw. I don't find Mother Berangu. I don't find Jinggaya. I hope they run away good, hide in bush.

They hide in bush at night, I don't find them. I call out, "Coo-ee" with long Coo and short ee like whip-bird call. Everybody in my mob know my cooee. Any one of my mob hear that, they give me cooee back.

I listen.

No cooee come back.

Either they don't hear me or they too scared call back. Or maybe they all dead except me. Maybe I only one alive.

I walk out of that camp into bush. I don't like stay in that camp with all them dead feller. I know I can't go near that camp again. That camp now proper bad place. I think, maybe I light fire, keep warm. Maybe light of fire help other feller find me. Light of fire keep *mamu* away. But then I think, maybe white feller see that light of fire. I don't want white feller see light of fire. I got to hope them *mamu* don't know where I sleep. I lie down on bed of gum leaves, pull branch over me, curl up small. That night get cold. I got no fire, I got no woman or any other feller lie next to, keep warm. I shiver.

I think, I got to send out my *yowi* find out what happen to Jinggaya and Mother Berangu and Monanggu and Nawngnaw. I think proper hard, get my *yowi* out of that *mulowil* and into that *dowi*. Oh! That *dowi* full of spirit. Them spirit run about, them spirit wild, them spirit angry. Them spirit run up to me, call out, ask me why so many feller got to be killed dead. I don't know what go on. I say to them, do you know *yowi* of Jinggaya? But them spirit don't answer, they beat their heads with stones, they angry and sad same time.

I find spirit of Goanna in that *dowi*. I ask Goanna, do you know where that *yowi* of Jinggaya? Of Berangu? Of Monanggu? Of Nawngnaw? Goanna turn his head one side, look at me out of one eye. He say nothing. That eye don't blink. He say nothing. Then I see that Goanna got water come from his eye. That Goanna too sad speak to me. He show me he proper unhappy. I know, my brother Goannas get killed dead, now Goanna got to mourn their death. I call out loud in that *dowi*, will no one tell me what happen to Jinggaya?

Now that *dowi* get like there some storm in him. All them spirit swirl round, run about quick like leaves stirred by strong wind. I feel my *yowi* get caught up in that wind, get blown about like leaf. I get blown here, I get blown there, I get giddy from blown about. I blown to dark corner of *dowi*. There I stop. I get held down while all them other spirit get blown about nearby. This dark corner quiet. I know I don't come here by chance, something bring me here, something hold me in that corner.

I look about. I see a man proper small in that corner. As I look he get bigger and bigger, then he stand with me and hold my arm. Cabba's dad! I speak his name and he smile at me. "Uncle," I say excited and surprised. "Uncle! Are you alive?"

He hold my arm proper soft. He put his face right near me and I see that smile a sad smile as well as a happy smile. He speak to me quiet. "Yes, Bradek, I alive. I glad see you alive too. So many of our mob dead. All their spirit here unhappy, they don't learn live spirit life yet, they angry lose their bodies. I live by run to trees. You live by run to trees too?"

"Yes, Uncle. I hear your call. You call 'Run to trees!'. I run to trees proper quick. Why so many of our mob slow run to trees?"

"Bradek, nephew, you clever man now. You know my *yowi*, you hear my thought good even when you don't hear my voice. That my thought you hear in that valley. Too much noise of shouts from our feller and from shouts of white feller and from them horse for hear my voice. You clever, you hear my thought, you run. Other feller not so clever, don't hear thought, don't run."

"Uncle, tell me, do you know if Jinggaya live? Or my children? Or Mother Berangu?"

Cabba's dad sign no. "I don't know anything about them. This *dowi*, I never know him like this before. Everything stirred up. Take long time before him calm, I think. Can't find anything when *dowi* like this."

"How you find me, then?"

197

Cabba's dad has kind smile in eyes. "Nephew, I go to tree layer of *dowi*. I go to that layer where spirit of trees live. Much calmer in that layer. Them tree spirits always proper gentle. They don't rush about like man spirit. They take all time they need. I ask them tree spirits, who hide our feller from the man-beast? I ask them, where the feller you look after so good? Them trees good friend of man. Them tree spirits bring me to this place, where I find you lost."

"Oh, Uncle, I so glad know you live! Your words right. Them trees my good friend, they look after me, hide me from the man-beast. I thank those trees for shield me! And I thank Mother Berangu for save me too!

"How Mother Berangu save you?"

"Oh, she wise woman! I learn wait patient from her, I learn wait long time when other feller give up. I wait patient in them trees that look after me so good. I wait until man-beast go."

"That Mother Berangu, she good woman. She good to me when I child, she good to all children in our mob. I know she know a lot of them secret only man got to know, but I don't say anything. She got a lot of wisdom, that woman. I wish she here help me now."

I surprised hear Cabba's dad need help. I don't think he ever need help before. I say, "Why, Uncle? What help you need from Berangu?"

He look at me with kind eyes. I see he got water in

them eyes. I see that water run down his cheeks. He fall on knees and cover his face with his hands. He don't like me see that water. "Oh, Bradek!" he say. His voice got a lot of trouble in him. "Oh, Bradek! You don't know what trouble I got!" His voice change to voice he use ask for big thing, same time he shake with sadness. "Help me, Bradek! Help me in my trouble!"

Me? Me help Cabba's dad? How this possible? I the feller need help. I say, "Uncle, how I help you?"

He grip my arms with his hands but he keep look to ground. He grip me tight. "Bradek, I lose my son in that battle! My son Cabba killed dead! I see him dead in that valley. Oh, Bradek, I see his head one place, his body another!"

When he say this, I remember I see that same thing. Horror! How I talk to Cabba's dad and not remember that? I so full of my own trouble I forget other feller got trouble too. I think, once more you stupid, Bradek.

I kneel down in front of Cabba's dad so he can see my face if he want. "Oh, Uncle," I say, "I see him too. I see so many bad things in that valley, and in our camp, too. Cabba, he was my initiation brother. I love him like my own brother. We play together as children, we hunt together as men. You lose a proper good son. I sorry."

I want say more but can't find words. We both quiet a bit. Then Cabba's dad say in voice that shake, "He was a proper good son, that true.

Bradek, tell me, do I do wrong in that battle? Do I kill my own son? Do I kill my brothers and sisters and sons and daughters? All them feller that mob, they all my family. Bradek, I got bad feeling, all them feller dead all my fault. Tell me, Bradek, do I do wrong?"

Now I see. Cabba's dad feel guilt for all them dead feller. If I Cabba's dad, maybe I feel same way. All them feller ask Cabba's dad what they got to do. He got to answer them. Now he not sure he answer right.

"Uncle," I say, "what else we do? We do nothing, them white feller take our land. Their sheep run all over our land, eat our grass. We got no land, we got no woman tucker gather from land. We got no grass, we got no kangaroo or emu for man hunt. We don't fight them white feller we all die for no tucker. I think you tell us do only thing we can."

Cabba's dad look in my face and I see his eyes thank me for say this. But same time I look in his face and I get this thought from him: maybe Bradek say this only for comfort.

Cabba's dad proper troubled. I think, I got to help him get over this trouble. He got to think about what do next, not what do last. I say to him, "Uncle, this valley, this camp near Goanna Rock, we never go there again. He bad place now, all them dead feller about, all them white feller on the land, all them sheep. You got to think about where you go now."

Cabba's dad sign yes. 'First I look about this bush, see if I can find any of our feller still alive. Then I think I go north, join up with them Guring-badawah. I got plenty family in them Guring-badawah, they let me join them. They take you too. You come with me?"

'Oh, Uncle," I say, "maybe I can't go with you. I got to search for Jinggaya and my children. First I got to search round camp, same like you. I don't find them I got to search out that Nose-Bone country way. I know my own mother dead. I don't know if my own father alive or dead. Maybe my own father hide in bush near camp, maybe you take him to Guringbadawah if he still alive?"

'I do, nephew," he say. "Now I got to go." And I feel that wind blow my *yowi* out of that *dowi* and I wake up. Through the trees that stand over me I see some of them stars fade. Sun Woman come soon. I got to get up and search for my family.

In camp, I find Cabba's dad. What he do, I don't know. He squat where his fire burn day before, look at ashes. I don't see his wives. I don't see his children. I go near him, he don't look up. I ask him if he see his family, he don't look up. Then he say in voice like voice of ghost, 'I think my family near. Don't know where exact, but I hope they safe, they come here by and by. My wives, I think they run off into bush with my children. I hope they safe. They come back by and by. I wait."

He say all this in voice like wind blow through she-oak trees, like man still asleep. I only see his eyes from side, but they not normal. Why not normal? Not sure. Maybe they don't blink like normal. I think, this man not normal.

I say, "You see Jinggaya? You see Mother Berangu or my children?"

He sign no. "Don't know about them," he say. He still don't look up. I think, he got private thoughts, I leave him.

I look all about camp. I find footprints of Jinggaya, but these old prints from before they leave camp. I find footprints of Berangu, Monanggu and Nawng-naw where they leave camp day before, but I can't follow them prints, they don't make good track. I think, maybe Berangu out in bush, got my children safe. Maybe she tie grass on feet so white feller don't track. Maybe she take them children over Nose-Bone way. Where Jinggaya? Maybe she lie dead in valley. Maybe she escape, look for me. Maybe she look for Berangu and children or run off Nose-Bone way like I say.

I know I got to go back to that valley. Don't want to, but got to know Jinggaya alive or dead. I go back. Before I get to valley I see them eagles fly round over head, hear call of crows, remind me what in valley. I start shake all over, can't help him, don't want go back but got to. I get to edge of trees, see down that valley, see eagles pick at them bodies wherever they got wound, see crows wait their turn when eagles finish. I walk along edge of trees, hear

202

sound of flies buzz in long grass. I find woman dead in grass. I know that woman, she not Jinggaya. I search all through them trees and all in that long grass. Easy find them bodies this day, each one got flies show me the way. I search and find plenty women. I know them women, but they not Jinggaya. I find plenty places where blood fall and no body near, or where bits of skin or hair left on tree show feller crash through. I think, some feller run off this way, maybe wounded. Maybe Jinggaya get wound, run off. I search all round them places in that valley, don't find her.

When I sure them white feller not there, I give my cooee proper loud all over that valley. There no answer. Nobody alive in that valley.

When Sun Woman get low in sky, I see smoke come from over our camp way. Not dark like smoke for signal, more light like smoke from fire at wurly. I run up there. I hope this fire mean Jinggaya come back. But when I get to camp, I find this smoke come from fire lit by Cabba's dad. He still the only feller in that camp. I ask him if any feller come. He say no, but he think his wives and children come back to that camp soon. Now he just wait, make sure he there for when they come back. He make fire as evening come so he keep warm that night.

"You sleep in camp here, then, with all these dead feller in camp?" I ask.

He say, "I got to stay here, be here for when my wives come back. Don't want sleep near all them dead feller but got to. Got to light fire keep *mamu* away. Now you help me. Help me bury them dead feller who lie in camp."

We take digging sticks and waddies and axes and dig up big bit of land near where our women dig yams. Cabba's dad say he don't think our mob ever come back to this place even if some of them live, so don't need them yams now. Ground good and soft for easy dig here. We dig him a bit, then drag them two old men and three old women into that place. We put them next to each other. Then we get them children and babies who lie in camp. We put them at heads of them old feller like they sleep in wurly. My feet say they don't want walk near them dead children and babies, my hands say they don't want pick them up. I got to talk strong to my feet and hands, make them do these things.

When all them dead feller in that place, we scrape the earth back over them. That earth don't cover them much. We stick their digging sticks and waddies in ground near. My eyes don't see them bodies under that earth, but I know they there. Their spirit hang over that earth, wonder what do. Their spirit thank me for let their bodies rest in dark like sleep. I know their spirit hang round that place long time, not know what do, but now I bury their bodies I know them spirit not angry with me. I talk about this with Cabba's dad. He say same.

"What we do about all them bodies in the valley?" I ask him. We squat round his fire in dark. We chew on a bit of damper we find in camp.

Cabba's dad pick up stick and scratch ground while

he think. "We can't bury all them feller," he say. "Too many." He say this while he look at ground and I see his eyes still don't blink right and he still not normal. I see him take big breath and let him out with shudder like a man cry, but he don't cry. "No, we got to let them stay in that valley. Their spirit proper unhappy have all them eagle eat their flesh and not bury their bodies proper, but can't help. This whole valley, all our country, him a place where no happy spirit stay now. This bad place for all time now. We don't come back here."

We both sleep in wurly belong Cabba's dad that night. We lie up against each other for keep out cold of the night. I don't sleep good, my mind full of troubles. In morning, Cabba's dad squat at fire again. He wait patient for his wives come back. I go out, pick up some fire wood for him, put him down near fire. He sign thank you. I say I got to go look for Jinggaya out Nose-Bone way. He sign he understand. I leave him still look at ground near that fire. He don't speak. He still don't blink like normal man.

*

I run on that track across Mairkaioo country towards Nose-Bone country. No Mairkaioo in sight. Maybe they off down the south of their country. Maybe they got their own troubles.

I look out for sign of Jinggaya or Berangu and children. Don't expect see much, for there plenty different way across that Mairkaioo country. I go the way first go when run off with Jinggaya. My

205

mother-in-law. This thought hit me like waddy again while I run. I run off with my mother-in-law. Can't think of a worse crime in my mob. Maybe this why I got so many troubles? I get punish for marry my mother-in-law? While I run I feel like I got cloud round head.

I don't carry any tucker so I got to stop a bit for gather some berry, find caterpillar in bark, dig root. Next day I reach hills at edge of Mairkaioo country. There only one way I know through them hills into Nose-Bone country. If I see sign of Jinggaya, I see him here.

Near foot of hills I look about for sign of Jinggaya. There some soft ground near that place. I see that soft ground. I look at that soft ground. Ai! I see a footprint I know in that soft ground! I see where foot arch, where toes come together, where side of foot run. Footprint of strong woman who walk smooth. That footprint remind me first time I see my mother-in-law. Jinggaya! She pass this way not long before.

I look careful at that ground. There something strange about that footprint. I think, what strange about that footprint? Why he remind me of first time meet my mother-in-law? Then I know why. That footprint of person who don't run or walk. That footprint put down careful, for leave sign. Jinggaya leave me sign she come this way.

I look again at footprint. I see other prints. I see where Jinggaya come, walk about, stand, put her good print down careful in soft earth. She put that print over some other mark in earth. That mark size of footprint but not shape of foot. That mark got lines and ridges across him. I know that mark! That the mark left by feller who walk with grass tied on feet. Can this be old mark left by Jinggaya and me when we run to Nose-Bone country? No, he too fresh. I look about more. I find more of them marks. I find more of same mark where feller walk. Nearby I find other marks made by smaller feet. Then I know! These got to be marks of Mother Berangu and my children! That old woman, she clever, she tie grass on all their feet so white feller don't know where they go. Jinggaya, she see these marks, she put her footprint on top careful, show me she come later. So Berangu pass this way with children. Then Jinggaya pass this way. Now I pass this way! We all go to Nose-Bone country. I jump up and down, I so happy know all these things. Then I run on up into them hills after my family.

When I get to that Nose-Bone country, there no sign of them Nose-Bones. No sign of Jinggaya. I run along through their wet land, see nothing. Then strange smell come to me. I know that smell. I smell him too often. I smell him in that Googerak camp, I smell him in my own mob camp.

I wade careful through bed of reeds. Before me come muddy bank which lead to grass and trees. I know this place, him a place them Nose-Bone come for rest or for children play by river. He got water and shade from trees. I keep behind reeds, for I see feller lie under them trees. They smell like dead feller.

I watch them feller. They don't move. I scared they all dead. I think maybe them white feller kill them all dead. I hide in them reeds, keep still, look all around for white feller. I stay in them reeds long time, don't see or hear anything like them white feller. By and by I come out of reeds, wade closer to bank. Now I see them feller better. They all Nose-Bone feller, some I know. All kind of feller lie dead there, old feller, young feller, child, man, women. There plenty dead feller lie in them trees, maybe count like fingers of two hands.

I get closer. They all covered in flies. I see they dead long time, their flesh all full of worms. I run on, get away from that place quick.

There plenty flood down towards Nose-Bone camp where I live with Jinggaya before. On way I find two more lots of them Nose-Bone feller on banks. They dead long time too, same like before. I proper scared, I think maybe them white feller kill all the feller in the world.

Then I get to Nose-Bone camp. He proper quiet, not many feller about. I run to Daingumbo wurly. I see Daingumbo first time, I proper happy see my friend. I see him lie on his side near his fire outside his wurly. I run up, shout, 'Ho! Daingumbo! Here your brother, Nantoomana!"

He don't get up. He roll on his back look up at me with big smile. He wave his hands and he look at me, but same time he look like he don't see me good. "Ho! Nantoomana!" he say. He say this in strange way, like he got lazy tongue. And then he start laughing.

I don't see what he laugh at. I don't see why he don't get up. "Are you crook?" I ask.

"Crook? No, I never so good, brother," he say with lazy tongue, and he laugh a lot more. I laugh too, I glad see him happy.

"You see Jinggaya?" I ask. I got to know this first.

"Jinggaya? Yes, yes, she here," he say and laugh more.

"Where? Where? She alive?"

"Alive? Alive!" he say like he talk to himself and start laugh again. "Yes, she alive!" He lift arm and point to bush, but he don't point steady. His arm wave all over that bush way. "She out there with Dilboong! They gone for woman tucker."

Hard hear what Daingumbo say, that tongue so lazy. I squat down near him, say quiet in voice with no laugh, "You sure you not crook, brother? You don't seem good. You don't seem steady."

"Steady?" he say. "I steady as any feller." Then he start get up. He sit up, then roll on side, then try stand, but fall into dirt face down. I hear him say to dirt, "I steady as any feller." Then he laugh more.

I watch him for a bit, see what he do next. But he

stay lie in the dirt. I go closer, look at him good. His face look like he get hit. His eyes shut. He breathe deep. He asleep! I think, how he fall asleep like that? He got to be crook, too right.

While I wait, I hear sound of footstep in bush. I jump up quick. Then voice call out, "Bradek! Bradek!" How much I want hear that voice! Jinggaya come run out of trees. She throw down her woman tucker and throw herself at me. "Oh, Bradek!" She got her arms round my neck, she cover me with kiss kiss. I put my arms round her, give her big hug. She give me more kiss kiss. "Oh, Bradek!" I pull her head back for look at her face, I see she got water in eyes. I laugh. I so happy, I get water in eyes too. We hug good. I hug her off ground, swing her round I so happy. You happy man that moment, Bradek, you most happy man in world.

Dilboong come up behind her. She carry a coolamon full of tucker. "Dilboong!" I say. "I happy see you too!" She give big smile. Then she look down at Daingumbo who still sleep. She put down coolamon, go up to Daingumbo, stir him with her toes.

"Get up, get up, you no use feller," she call. Daingumbo stir a bit but he don't get up.

"What his trouble?" I ask. Before she answer I ask Jinggaya, "You seen Monanggu and Nawngnaw?" Can't wait for one answer before next question, got to know all them answers proper quick.

Dilboong and Jinggaya both speak same time. Dilboong say something about white feller, Jinggaya say, "No, I don't see them. You don't see them?" I got to sign her no, and I hug her for comfort. She ask, "What happen at camp? I see many feller killed down the valley, I hear you shout I got to run."

"All them feller dead, Jinggaya."

She got troubled look. "All dead? Your own mother, your own father? Cabba? Borrudum? All dead?" I got to tell her they all dead. She ask about many other feller. I got to tell her they all dead too. She look so weak I think she fall to ground. I hold her up, give her comfort. Then she ask in feeble voice, "How you get away?"

I tell her I run to trees, hide from white feller. "Other feller run to trees too, I think some of them still about, but I don't see them. Only feller I see is Cabba's dad. All them other feller dead or run off. How you escape?"

Dilboong shout at Daingumbo. I hear her say something about white feller again. "What you say, Dilboong?" I ask.

Jinggaya say, "I run when I hear your call. Other women slow to run. I reach trees, see them white feller hit them with sticks. Now I know them sticks like sharp knife, cut through a body. I know I can't cross that valley find out what happen to you, then I remember you tell Berangu run for Nose-Bone country, so I run this way. You see them tracks of grass on feet?"

"Get up, no use feller," shout Dilboong.

"I think they tracks of Berangu and our children," I tell Jinggaya.

"Them white feller, they give him drink," say Dilboong.

"What white feller?" I ask, proper scared.

"Berangu don't come this way," say Jinggaya. "Maybe she see all them dead feller, go away from this place."

"How all them feller die?" I ask.

"White feller come here all time," say Jinggaya. "Not like them white feller come our way. These white feller come, give axe, give knife, take spear, take throwing stick. They bring white feller tucker too."

Dilboong say, "All them feller our mob, they all get crook and die. Many, many die. We all get crook, I get crook, look." She point to her face. I see she got scabs on her face.

"Daingumbo do that?" I ask.

She give sneer laugh. "That Daingumbo don't do anything! No, we all get crook, we get skin trouble, this skin all bulge up in spots, break out, lots of stuff come out. Lots of our feller die. I get him, Daingumbo get him. We don't die. Now we got scabs on spots. We get scar by and by, you see."

"Tell me what trouble Daingumbo got now."

"Huh! He got white feller drink trouble."

I look at Jinggaya, see if she explain better. She say, 'These white feller, they bring drink they call grog. They give that grog to Daingumbo. Daingumbo give Dilboong to them white feller for keep peace. This happen many time. That drink, that grog, he like *pituri*. Make mind wild, make body sleep. Dilboong say he taste like wombat piss, but Daingumbo he drink him plenty. That his trouble now."

"This true?" I ask Dilboong. "Daingumbo give you to white feller?"

She sign yes. She sign she don't care. 'They more use than him, too right they are. His cock fall off soon, he forget how use him."

Jinggaya pass me some woman tucker and I remember I hungry. I stuff mouth, hold Jinggaya and talk same time. 'These white feller don't kill Nose Bones, then? You see these white feller?"

Jinggaya sign yes. 'I hide in trees when white feller come. Daingumbo, Dilboong, they speak to white feller. He don't kill Nose Bones. But he got stick that shout, like them feller kill all our mob. I see them stick, he shout with them stick at duck and kangaroo, kill them dead long way off. He got long stick for shout feller long way off, short stick for shout feller near. He call that long stick musket, he call that short stick pistol."

"My head hurt with all this," I say. "Are we safe here?"

Jinggaya still hug me. 'Yes, I think we safe. Them

white feller go away for a bit now, I think. They not same like white feller come to our valley, they don't kill any of this mob."

"I don't like, anyway. Now Sun Woman go down, we got to stay here tonight. But first light we got to go search for Berangu and children."

Jinggaya's arms stroke up and down my back. She say, "I miss you, Bradek."

I don't feel so hungry now. I stroke her back. "I miss you, too right I do," I say and let her lead me to our wurly.

Daingumbo different feller next morning. He get up, he more steady. He rub his eyes a lot, hold his head a lot, he speak in thick voice but not with lazy tongue. He make groan. "Uuugh! My head hurt!" Then he look at me with smile and say, "Good see you, brother."

I tell him about white feller kill our mob, how we come here. He tell me about white feller come to his camp, bring grog, want woman. He tell me about many Nose Bone die from that bursting spot. He say he get good life, don't need hunt, them white feller bring plenty tucker, they bring meat called beef taste as good as emu. He say that grog make him feel good, make him forget all trouble, forget all them feller die of bursting spot. He say I got to try him, but he got to wait for more grog come, maybe today.

I don't want meet white feller, drink white feller grog. I tell him we got to go, find Berangu and children. "They come over hills into Nose-Bone country all right," I say. "They don't come down here, or you see them. Which way you think they go?"

Daingumbo scratch his beard. "Hmm, I don't know," he say, "but hand of my father, he know!" He pull out that hand that still under his arm and point him to south. "No," he say. He point him to west. "No," he say. He point him east. "Hmm," he say. He point him north. "Hmm," he say again. Then he point him between east and north. I see that hand start shake. "That the way!" say Daingumbo. "Hand of my father say they go that way!"

*

I walk with Jinggaya between east and north. That land start flat, like most of Nose-Bone land, but slowly get higher. We travel quick when moving, but got to stop gather woman tucker and find water on way. This country not like our own country, not like Nose-Bone country, we don't know all them places animals hide in this country, so we got to make do with woman tucker. We get higher and higher, until after three days we see all that country lie below us, trees and grass and water. We see all over Nose-Bone country, right to them hills that lead back to our own country. We know we on other side of world now. I never know world so big. We see smoke from fire over Daingumbo camp way. We see other smoke far off. There feller in this country all right, but where Berangu and children?

"That could be Berangu," I say. I point to thin smoke rise in north.

"Why not that one?" ask Jinggaya. She point to smoke in south.

I sign I don't know. Jinggaya say, "They both far away. Do we go look, or keep go way hand of Daingumbo father say?"

I say, "That smoke in north far, take one day get there and back. Same for smoke in south. They not Berangu, we lose two days more, they further away."

Jinggaya agree. "I go find feller in south, you go find feller in north. Meet back here tomorrow, before Sun Woman go down. That way, we lose only one day."

This good plan. I say, "You find Berangu, you still come back here. I find Berangu, I still come back here." Jinggaya sign she understand. We make camp, for dark come. In morning we say goodbye, run off quick find them fires.

I run down to fire in north. I see small mob down that way, gather woman tucker. There one young man, two old women, three young women and some children. I watch them from behind trees. They don't see me. Then I show myself to young man from a distance. He look up quick, shout to women and children. They all hide in bush. That young man stay. I put down my spears, hold up fist. I see that young feller smile. He put down his spear, walk over my way. I walk to him.

When he close, I see his face and hands covered with scars. I think, this feller get them bursting spots some time back.

"You see old woman with two children, boy and girl, pass this way?" I ask.

He say something back to me. I don't understand much of his lingo. I sign, old woman, young boy, young girl, you see?

He sign yes! He see old woman, young boy, young girl!

Which way? I sign.

He point. He point up slope, between north and east! Hand of Daingumbo father tell truth!

How many days? I sign.

He think for a bit. Then he sign three. Three days only! They not far away.

I sign thanks, run back fast as I can. When I get back, Jinggaya already there wait for me. I tell her, "That mob in north, they see Berangu, only three day back! They say she go between north and east! We hurry, we catch them up!"

"Oh, Bradek," say Jinggaya. "This good news. We got to hurry now, catch up with Berangu and children. I want see my children so bad."

"Why you back so quick?" I ask.

"I get down near that fire, I see him fire belong white feller camp. There man-beast, down there, white feller, horse. There sheep down there too. I know Berangu don't go that way. She don't go anywhere near white feller. I turn back quick."

Next morning we hurry up that slope. From top we see more ranges of hills, go long way, all covered in trees. Don't see much smoke. This hard. A feller can look long time in this country not find his family.

After two days we come to river. He big river, too deep for wade across. We think, some mob live near this river, too right. We follow river bank. Plenty mud and sand beside that river, plenty footprint, but we don't see footprint of Berangu. By and by we see canoe on other bank of river. Feller fish from that canoe. I see he got fish spear. Mullet jump out of water, maybe they catch fly, maybe they got some feller after them. I see this feller wait for mullet jump, then spear him with fish spear. He get two mullet while we watch from behind trees. He good spear man.

We see him look at trees. We hide, but he know we there. He got good beard and bone through nose, but he not Nose Bone mob I know. He stand in canoe and call out to us in strange lingo. His voice sound like voice of friend. I tell Jinggaya keep back. I show myself, plant spear, give peace sign. Feller in that canoe give me smile. He sign, where you from?

I sign, over hills. I sign, you see old woman with two children pass here?

He sign, old woman with limp?

Oh joy! He see Berangu. I sign, how many days?

He sign, two.

Which way?

He point up river on his side.

We cross here?

He sign, yes.

I call Jinggaya and I see that feller smile again. Don't blame any feller smile see Jinggaya, she good looking woman. I tell Jinggaya wait while I swim over, don't want both in water same time. Then I swim over with my spears and shield and stand near that feller. When I stand close I see as well as scar all over made by feller he got scar on face from them spots. He smile. He got no weapon, only fish spear. I think, he peaceful feller. I call Jinggaya come over.

This feller say his name Maulan. I give him Bradek for my name. He got camp nearby, through trees. He ask, we hungry? Too right we are!

We go through trees to his camp, meet his family. I never see feller with so many scar. They make them scar with sharp edge of mussel shell. Cut long line, fill him with stuff, make proper proud scar. They got them scar all over. I think my scar look like boy scar, they got man scar! On top of them scar, they got scar from them bursting spots.

They got good tucker. They got fish, they got berry, they got root, they got possum and lizard. We cook them fish, eat plenty. I think, this good mob. I don't see much scar on them from fight, they all happy. They sing their mob song. They got good life by this river. I get big fish bone, put him through my nose, show I nose bone feller like them. They all clap and laugh when I do this. I happy be with that mob.

Then I see something give me trouble. Near wurly belong Maulan an axe lie on grass. I think, I know that axe. He that cold grey axe come with white feller. I sign Maulan, white feller come, give axe?

He sign, white feller come, give axe, give knife, give string, give tucker.

I sign, they bring stick that shout, kill dead? Stick that cut off head?

He sign, they got them sticks, kill kangaroo, emu, duck. They eat all that tucker. They kill crow, eagle. They give that tucker to Maulan. They eat good tucker, Maulan get bad tucker.

I sign, where them white feller?

He sign, they got camp one day walk off. He sign, some women from this mob go to white feller camp, keep peace.

We sleep a bit after eat. When wake, I think time we

look for Berangu. Jinggaya say she feel crook. I say, maybe this tucker she eat no good, but she say, no, she feel crook before but don't like say.

I feel her head. She hot, she got fever. I look at her skin. She got red mark come on skin round neck. I say, "You crook all right. We got to find herb for fix this."

I call Maulan. I sign, Jinggaya crook, need herb.

He look at her close. Then he step back, look at me. He sign, this woman crook with bursting spot. He come soon.

My Jinggaya say, "I got to go on. I got to find my children." I see she want go, but feel crook.

I sign Maulan what Jinggaya say. I think, maybe Jinggaya got to stay here, I go on alone.

Maulan sign back, that woman too crook for walk. He sign, soon Bradek get bursting spot too. He sign, crook feller out back too weak find water, gather tucker. He die from thirst or hunger. He sign, stay this place, we get tucker, maybe Bradek and woman live. Then he sign, many feller in his mob get bursting spot, many die in camp.

I tell all this to Jinggaya except the last bit. She slip to ground, start cry. I say, "I don't know what else do."

She say, "I know, Bradek. You do all you can. I sad not see my children. Can't help him, that all. Now we both get crook."

I squat beside her, stroke her arm. "When we better, we go straight find them children, you see. We know they pass this way. Maulan mob gather tucker all round here, they tell us if them children come back this way. Them children go further on, we catch them some day."

She sign she know this, but she still look sad. I try comfort her. "We lucky fall in with this mob. They proper good mob. They feed us, they fetch water for us, make fire. They look after us. We don't have this mob look after us, we die pretty damn quick."

Maulan mob come in from gather tucker. Not many left in that mob. Only two men left, they got three wives each. Them wives widows of other men who die from bursting spot. Some of them widows still got their heads covered with clay caps for mourn their husbands. Each of them women look after two children. All that mob come over to me and Jinggaya, sign welcome, offer tucker. I so happy meet that kind mob. I think, why some mob fight stranger, send him away? This mob welcome stranger. This better way. Then I think back to my old mob. I think, maybe we don't fight stranger but we don't welcome him as good as Maulan mob. I think, when stranger come to my old mob, maybe we give him a bit of water and a bit of tucker, but we watch him careful, we don't trust until we know him better. This mob belong Maulan, they trust me and Jinggaya. They treat us like we belong their family. I feel shame when I think of this. Meet that mob belong Maulan, him one of the good things in my life.

Jinggaya fever come hot that night. She shiver, cry out, shake all night. I sit by her, give her water, try keep her cool when she hot, warm when she cold. She shiver and shake. She don't know who I am. She don't know where she is. I think, maybe my Jinggaya die like all them other feller. She lie on possum skin rug. I feel that rug, him wet like water pour on him. I think, Jinggaya don't have that much water in her, but she still sweat in that fever.

Before morning I fall asleep next to that woman. When I wake, first light of dawn show at entrance of wurly. I see Jinggaya lie next to me. She still, very still. I touch her. She cold! She so very cold! I think, my Jinggaya, she die! I cry out and weep over her. Oh! Jinggaya, don't die!

Maulan run into wurly when he hear my shout. He squat beside Jinggaya, touch her neck. He sign, this woman not dead. He sign, keep her warm. He sign, this woman got to be smoked.

I lie beside Jinggaya, give her my warmth, and cover her up with roo skin. Same time I hear Maulan talk outside, tell other feller in his mob what do. I see them make big fire, then spread embers on ground. They cover them embers with plenty green grass and green leaf so he proper smoky. When he proper smoky, they come for Jinggaya, lay her on that grass and cover her with more grass so she smoked good. I see that smoke stroke her body all over and I know that smoke do her good. After a bit she cough in that smoke and I glad see her alive. Then that Maulan mob take Jinggaya out of that smoke and put her back in wurly. They sign to me, soon bursting spot come.

Jinggaya open her eyes, look at me. I think she know me now, but she so weak. She too weak lift her own arms. I pull her head up a bit in my arm and give her a bit of water from a coolamon. She look at me and give me a smile. How I love that smile! He don't last long that time, but he warm me all over. Then Jinggaya fall asleep, even before I put her head down.

Maulan bring me some tucker. He sign, bursting spot come soon. He sign, got to wait, nothing else can do. He squat at entrance to wurly. He teach me some of their lingo. I soon got a few words. He laugh when I learn good, clap hands. He laugh when I make mistake. He like laugh a lot. I like this Maulan feller, he good feller. He spend all rest of day by that wurly, give water and tucker, help me learn his lingo.

That night, I get that fever. I get hot like Jinggaya get hot. I don't know much what happen. I remember Maulan sit beside me, try cool me with water on head. I remember lie on possum skin, he cold and wet from my sweat. But I don't remember much what happen outside my body that night. I remember what happen in my mind though.

In my mind I back in that valley belong my old mob. I see them man-beast raise their sticks and shout at all them men in my mob. I see all them men fall to ground. I see them man-beast run up with sharp stick, slash at them men. I see them man-beast slash at our women, see our women fall to ground. I see them man-beast cut off heads and cut throats and cut bodies. I see all that, I feel proper crook after see all that. Then I see what happen all from beginning again, from the time them man-beast come up that valley and all our men go out in a line meet them with our spear. I see all them man-beast raise their stick again, shout again, see our men fall again, our women fall, see them sticks slash and cut. And what I see, I see again and again that night. I think maybe I die and my spirit got to see this again and again for all time.

After this, I don't know much. Next thing I know, I lie in that wurly. Sun Woman shine outside, but shady in wurly. Jinggaya lie next to me. She lie on her side, got head on arm. She say quiet, "Bradek, you awake?"

"Unghm." Seem I don't speak too good. I feel weak.

"Oh, Bradek, you come back to me!" I feel her touch, I feel her pull herself closer. I feel her tears fall on my cheek.

Maulan come, lift my head in his arm and give me water, same like I do for Jinggaya before. I open my eyes, look about. I see Jinggaya. She got spot come all over face. I say, "You got spotty face!"

"Ha!" she laugh. "I got spotty face, I got spotty hands, I got spotty feet! You get him soon."

225

"What happen?" I ask. "I don't know what happen."

"You get fever. Maulan look after you all night. In morning, he smoke you, bring you back here. You sleep whole day whole night. That Maulan good feller. We don't have Maulan, we dead now, I think."

"Too right," I say. Too weak say much.

Later I take a bit of tucker, sit up a bit. I see Jinggaya better. Her spots full of clear stuff, like blister, but all over her face. "I know him look bad," she say, "but I feel better now than with fever."

Next day them spots come to me. Spots belong Jinggaya go yellow. They grow so big they join up at edges. Her face like one big yellow spot.

More days pass with these spots. We too crook go anywhere, but we don't feel we die like with fever. Sometimes Maulan come sit with us, sometimes other feller from his mob. They keep our fire going, bring us water, bring us tucker all these days.

My spots go yellow like spots belong Jinggaya. She look at me, say she never see anything so horrible before.

More days after, her spots turn into scab. Her whole face like one big scab. She got scabs all over hands and feet too.

I say to Jinggaya, "At least one good thing come from this."

She say, "What that? What good thing come?"

I say, "You get your wish."

She say, "I get my wish? What wish that?"

I say, "Don't you remember? When we talk that time we lie hurt in Nose-Bone country? I tell you I like you beautiful. You tell me you wish you ugly? Well, you ugly now! You most ugly woman I ever see!"

I see her start laugh, same time water come from eyes. She say, "Don't make me laugh! These scabs all crack and peel, you make me laugh! You wait, you get him by and by!"

I do too, but when scabs come I start feel strong again. We start help that mob belong Maulan, gather firewood, look for tucker. We learn some more of their lingo. I say to Maulan, "You good feller. You look after us good. All this mob belong Maulan, good feller."

He look like he don't want me say this. He say, "I get sick, you do same."

I think, I wish that true. Maybe next time, I do like Maulan. Then I say to him, "We got to go find our children."

He look sad. He say, "You good feller, Bradek. Your woman good woman. Our mob need more feller. Many of our mob die with bursting spot. You find your children, you come back here, join our mob. We want you join our mob."

Me and Jinggaya proper happy hear this. I tell Maulan something of what happen to my old mob. He shocked. He say, "We don't get that here. Them white feller, we don't like much, they want our women, but they don't give us much trouble."

I say, "I hope that true all time."

Next morning, me and Jinggaya leave that camp look for our children. All that mob line up with sad faces, say they hope we come back. We feel proper sad leave that place, we both got water in eyes as we walk off.

I don't tell you all that happen when we look for children. We walk over that country, always more north and more east. We walk over that country while moon come and go many times, then many times more. We walk over that country while three years come and go. We meet all kinds of mob, fall in with them, walk about with them, then move on. They all get that bursting spot some time, they all got lots of dead family. We meet some feller with mob get killed by white feller musket and pistol, same like my mob. Many of them mobs too small for get along, maybe they got no man can hunt or got no woman can have children. They walk about try meet up with other mob.

Every feller we meet, we ask "You see old woman with two children, boy and girl, pass this way?" Some say no, some say yes, maybe, but don't remember where go or when. We know we follow old trail, maybe too old.

We in new country. Not much tucker in this country. Some feller gather up all woman tucker in that country. We don't see these feller, maybe they move on. We get hungry.

We come to new place. All round that place there smoke from fires. Some big mob make camp round this place. They cover that place. But they don't camp like normal mob. Their wurlies all over the place, they made all kinds of different ways. They don't guard that camp, keep look out, like normal mob. They don't take any notice of us when we walk in. We see men, women, children squat round fires. Now I see they all different sort of feller, all come from different mob, gather here make one big mob. Some got short cut scars like mine, some got long cuts, some got burn scars; some got hair to shoulder like mine, some got him tied up, some got him in a net; some wear nothing like me, some got apron like Apron Man when we first see him, some got more covering over their bodies like them white feller; some wear feathers or necklace or arm band, some don't; some got nose bones, some don't. They all got plenty scar from them bursting spot though, same like me.

I say to Jinggaya, 'This strange mob. Strange smell too.'

She say, 'Yes, strange smell. What that smell?'

I think. Then I know. 'Horse,' I say.

We go round some of that place, ask about Berangu

and our children. No one know. We look out for them over that place, but don't see. This proper big camp, many place got to look. We meet a Goanna, he give us some tucker. This strange tucker he call beef and bread. That beef good, but we spit out that bread, he don't taste like tucker. This Goanna don't speak any lingo I know, but later we meet an old feller who got some lingo I know. He squat alone next to his fire. I ask him about this place.

"All these feller, they come from all round here," he say. "They lose their families to that bursting spot white feller call pox. Or their mob wiped out by them white feller, or their country taken by them white feller and they got no country left."

"How they all live?" I ask, for don't seem much tucker around that place. We don't see any kangaroo. On way in, we see all the berries and shoots and seeds picked before we get here.

He look at me like I stupid. "You just get here?" he ask. Then he turn and point out of that place. "Big mob of them white feller got a camp over there. They got horse and sheep and cow …"

I stop him with question. "What this cow? I see horse, I see sheep."

"Cow, him big beast, got no toes, same like sheep and horse. White feller drink milk of woman cow! Can you believe that? Drink milk of woman beast! White feller make man cow pull his things all over this country."

"Ah! Big beast, no toes! He got two tail he drag on

ground, make track?"

This old feller laugh. "Yes, he that beast," he say. "You see by and by. White feller eat meat of them cow, call him beef."

"Ah, beef! Brother Goanna here give me beef, he taste good."

"Yes," say the old feller, "he taste good. He get that beef from white feller. Them white feller got plenty beef, plenty other tucker. They got water come from hole in ground; not muddy water, good clear water. They got all the water and all the tucker any feller want. They got tea for drink too, and grog. They got axes and knives, they got nets, they got everything in their camp any feller want."

"And they give all this stuff to all this mob here?" I ask. I look around at all them feller camp there and I think, they can't all live on white feller tucker, not enough tucker anywhere for mob this big.

He laugh a bit. "Yes, they give. But don't give him to all. Some of these feller here, they go over that white feller country, stop dog from kill their sheep, bring back cow that wander off, do other thing white feller ask. White feller give them feller tucker, them feller share with us."

I say, "Them white feller bad feller. They kill all my old mob, take our country."

He look at me and sign he understand. He ask us squat at his fire. "You hungry?" he ask. "I got a little bit of tucker here, I share with you."

We proper hungry. We see that old feller get his tucker. Not much, even for old feller. We don't like eat his tucker. "Go on," he say, "eat him. I get more tomorrow. I got nephew look after white feller sheep."

We eat strange tucker, not bad. That old feller put strange coolamon on fire. He full of water. That coolamon don't burn. We watch while we eat. When that water inside hot, old feller throw in leaf, take coolamon off fire by hook him with stick. He add sand he take from dilly. Then he pass us coolamon. "Drink!" he say. "He good. This white feller tea."

We look in that coolamon. He got no sand we can see. We drink that white feller tea. He taste good, sweet like nectar.

I look about. "All these feller live from look after white feller sheep and cow?" I ask.

He sign yes, maybe.

I say, "I don't want go near them white feller. They bad feller. Where best place look for tucker?"

He look about. Then he say, "No tucker some days walk from this place. All that tucker gathered by this mob. No tucker round here now. Only white feller tucker, white feller water. You stay here, you got to eat white feller tucker."

I sign I don't like. He look at Jinggaya. Then he look at me. "Plenty women here go up that white feller camp. Them white feller got no women of their own. Woman who go up that white feller camp, she send back plenty tucker. Send back more tucker than all them men who look after sheep. Send back tucker, send back grog, send back axe, send back everything."

"My woman don't go to white feller," I say.

He don't look at me. Then he say to fire, "You see. Them white feller, they send Captain round camp, look for woman. That Captain bring grog, choose woman. He see your woman, he choose her. I know. Them white feller, they like your woman plenty good. You see. You stay here, you get plenty hungry by and by."

We make a wurly at edge of camp. We look for tucker and water, don't find. Don't find much firewood either. We sleep hungry and cold that night. Next morning we got to brush dew off grass for drink. We go on round camp, ask for Berangu, don't find. Some feller give us a little bit of tucker, but we hungry and cold again next night. Next day we finish go round that camp, see everything, see track go up to white feller camp, see their horse. Berangu and our children not in this place.

"We got to go on," say Jinggaya.

"Yes," I say. "I glad they not here. I don't like this place." I know my head hang down. I think I lose hope find children. "We stay here one more night. Tomorrow first light we go on. If anyone give tucker, save him. We got long walk no tucker if that old feller tell truth." I try say this happy, but I know

233

my voice sound tired and show I hide sadness.

Jinggaya look sad. Evening come, we get a few sticks make a fire. I see that fire gleam on water in her eyes. She don't look at me, she look far off. "Bradek," she say, "you think Berangu and our children dead?"

"No," I say in voice get stronger. "No! Berangu die, I know him. Too right I know him. No, they live! But where ..."

While we talk, two feller come over our way. They carry firestick in dark. I don't think much about this, carry on talk. But when they proper close, I see one of them feller got covering all over, got no feet, got head cover. White feller! I jump up and pull Jinggaya behind me. I got spear on ground, I grip him in my toes.

A black feller come with this white feller. He got some of them white feller covering. He step closer, say something in different lingos. Then he say something in lingo I know, I show I understand. He give me greeting in this lingo.

"This white feller, he Captain," he say. "He bring grog, tucker." He hold out things, show me that grog and tucker. I say nothing. I don't want grog, but I want tucker for I proper hungry. He see me not sure. He hold out a bit of tucker. This look like that beef. That feller step closer, hold him out more. I take that bit of beef, taste him. He taste good. I know this Captain want woman, but I think maybe trade spear instead.

That feller say, "Captain want your woman come up white feller camp."

I say, "My woman don't go white feller camp. I got good spear, I give him for tucker."

That feller speak to Captain and I see that Captain laugh. Then feller say, "No, Captain only want woman. He give plenty grog and tucker for woman." Jinggaya hide behind me, her hands on my waist. I feel her peer out round side, see what go on.

"No!" I say, and beat my chest. "My Goanna run up over that Captain!" I don't like these feller. "Tell Captain go away!" I wave my hand, show go away. I proper angry, proper scared same time.

I see that Captain put his hand in his body and pull out short stick. He point that stick at me. He shout me with pistol! I hear Jinggaya call out "No!" and jump out in front of me before I can stop her. I hear that Captain shout, I see his pistol breathe fire, I feel Jinggaya fall back on me. Same time, I pick up that spear with my toes, pass him to hand proper quick, throw him at that Captain! I see that spear go through neck of Captain! That spear go right through his neck, come out other side. I see that Captain drop his stick, drop his torch, grab that spear with both hands. I see that Captain step back, then fall over backwards onto ground. He still hold that spear. I see the eyes of that other feller big in the light of his torch. He hold that torch over Captain, then he hold up torch and look at me. He look proper scared. Then he turn and run off out across camp. He run off white feller camp way.

I hold Jinggaya. "Jinggaya, you all right?" I ask. I got bad fear she hurt.

"Yes, yes," she say. "I all right. You all right?"

"Yes," I say, "I all right." Same time I feel Jinggaya lean more against me, start slip down. "You sure you all right?" I turn her round so she face me and I see she got blood on her chest, just under collar bone. I touch that place, feel her warm blood on my fingers, see that blood run down her breast. "Jinggaya! That shout hurt you!"

"I all right," she say again. She look over her shoulder. That white feller still move his legs a bit, wriggle on that ground. "You kill that white feller! You kill him dead all right. Oh, Bradek, we got to leave this place quick! Them other white feller come here, they kill you dead, that for sure!"

I know this true, I know we got to get out of that place quick, even though that night all dark beyond the camp fires. We gather up all our things. I tie grass on our feet and add some of that blood from secret vein. Then I lead Jinggaya off into bush. I lead her into thick bush where white feller horse don't go, where no feller can see us. I give Jinggaya grass for her wound so no blood drip, leave trail. I know she hurt, for I hear her breathe hard behind me, and I got to help her often when we go up steep bits. We don't run, we go careful so don't disturb bush, leave trail. We keep travel through thick bush all that night, get well away from that white feller place. When morning come, we go over ridge, I find good cave in cliff face, only way in through ledge. I tell Jinggaya we hide in that cave in case white feller come after us.

We don't make fire, but that cave quite dry and he get warm when Sun Woman rise. I tell Jinggaya she got to sleep, for we leave when evening come and walk in the night again.

"Yes," she say. I see she got some pain, I see her wound don't bleed now. I look at that wound.

"I go find some herb and clay for that wound, make him better," I tell her.

"No," say Jinggaya, "don't take chance. Keep in cave where white feller don't see you. I all right."

I look at her. "I know you strong woman," I say, "but I still got to get medicine."

She grab my hand quick. "No, don't go. I all right. This true. But, Bradek," she say, with tight grip on my hand, "if I die, promise you carry on look for our children."

I look at her surprised. "You don't die," I say. "You can't die, you proper strong woman!"

"Yes, yes," she say. "But if I do die, promise me you look for our children. Just give me promise."

"Of course," I say. "I never stop look until I find them children."

She smile at me. Oh, how I love that smile! That

237

smile warm me like Sun Woman, make all trouble go. I smile back at her.

Then she close her eyes and she go to sleep.

I got to wake Jinggaya next evening. She sleepy, she say shoulder hurt a bit, but she ready go on, get safe. Her voice come like wind, she pant like she don't breathe good. She don't sound good. She say she know we got to go on, get safe. She ask if any water near. I got to say I don't know, don't see water near.

She don't get up. I stroke her head for comfort. That head! He burn like fire! I feel that head with palm of hand, he burn all right. Jinggaya got fever like with that pox. "You got fever," I say. "You too sick go on, got to rest here."

"No," she say, "got to go on, got to get safe." But I hear in her voice some thought say she not well enough for go on.

"No, we stay here. I don't see or hear them white feller all day. We safe in this place, we hide here good. We stay here, you rest, get better. I go find water."

I know best chance find water in this place at bottom of cliff and I got to hurry climb down while still light. I take coolamon, climb down that cliff. Not hard climb, plenty ledge and root for grip. At bottom of cliff I find another small cave. He got fern and moss grow all round roof. I look about, find place where water drip through top of that cave. I hold coolamon up, and he fill with water, but proper slow, one drop by one drop.

That climb back with coolamon proper hard. That night proper dark when I get back to cave. Can't see a thing inside. I feel my way back beside my Jinggaya. I think I wake her from sleep, for she don't say much. I pick up her head in my arm, give her little bit of water from coolamon.

She say, in proper quiet voice, "Bradek."

"Yes?"

"Bradek, I die, you find children?"

"You don't die, you don't die."

"Promise you find children."

"I promise. Now you sleep. You see, you better in morning."

Oh, Bradek, how wrong! When morning come, that woman proper crook. She don't move much, her breath come hard with rattle in throat. She don't know where she is. I lie beside her all that day, stroke her head, talk to her, but she don't open her eyes. I think, she slip away from me. Her breath less, her chest hardly move, I don't hear her breath. Oh Jinggaya, don't die! I call her name, stroke her but she don't answer. Jinggaya, please don't die! As evening come again I feel her get cold. I lie next to her, give her my warmth. She don't wake up. "Jinggaya, Jinggaya!" I say, but she don't answer.

As that cave get darker, she feel colder. Jinggaya! She don't answer. I can't warm her, I can't hear her breath. Jinggaya, don't leave me!

In the morning her body next to mine cold like stone. I know then that her spirit leave that body. I hold her head in my arms and cry my tears over her. That Jinggaya, she best woman man can ever know. She risk get killed dead run away with her son-in-law. She give her life save her husband. Now she lie dead without ever find her lost children. I hold her in that cave long time, remember all them things we do together.

*

I bury Jinggaya on top of that ridge. I plant her digging stick in ground by her head, that black wood digging stick I carve with Goanna and Black Cockatoo sign in Nose-Bone country. I sad she don't get proper burial like with my old mob, sad she don't get her family round her help rest her spirit. But when I look round that ridge, I see she got green valley either side, good country, a bit like that country round Goanna Rock back our way, and I think, Jinggaya spirit got all this country for roam, this beautiful country, maybe that spirit rest here not too bad.

Then I think, but that spirit of Jinggaya, he don't rest until Bradek find them children. Oh Monanggu! Oh Nawngnaw! Oh Jinggaya!

I stay about that place a few days, get proper hungry for no tucker there except a few grubs I find under bark. Then one evening when I stand next to place where Jinggaya lie, I look over that country and I see leaves stir on trees across valley. I watch them leaves stir in late light from Sun Woman, and I see tops of them trees sway. Some strong wind come up that valley, he sweep up that valley, stir all them trees. I see him blow leaves off them trees, all them leaves swirl up around that valley. I see twigs and branches get blown off, swirl around and fall down. Proper strong wind sweep up that valley. He come to my ridge, he blow on my face, he blow my hair back, and he shake all them trees on my ridge so them leaf swirl all around me. I think, this wind, he come from west and south. I smell that wind, and that wind tell me I got to go back to Goanna Rock, go back to my own country.

I think, maybe Berangu go back to old country. Maybe she go on. I don't know. I look for them children long time, got to keep on looking. Maybe I look in old country now. Maybe they there. I pick up my things, say goodbye to Jinggaya, tell her I always look for them children, and walk back towards my old country.

I don't tell you all about that journey. At that river where I meet Maulan I look out for that feller and his mob, but no one there. Maybe they go walk about. Maybe they all dead. I don't know.

In Nose Bone country plenty white feller, plenty horse, plenty sheep. I keep round that country. Don' t see Daingumbo or his mob. Maybe they go away. Maybe they in among them white feller. Maybe they all dead. I don't know.

When I get to my old mob country, I see them sheep at bottom of valley. I go round, keep behind trees. Then I go up our valley. I see tree I know, he greet me like old friend. All them trees, I know them all, every one of them wave his arm to me, say welcome home Bradek. I see rocks I know, they say welcome home Bradek. All the grass in that valley he grow long, for no one burn him. All that grass, he grow long, he hide everything on the ground. He hide the bones of my mob, he hide the bones of our warrior and our women that lie on that ground. I don't trouble them bones.

I get up to Goanna Rock. That sacred board still hide there, I get him out and sing for Goanna. That Goanna sign fade from not get painted. I make paint, paint him up again proper good. I sit on top of that rock and look out over our country.

A shout come to me. Bradek! A shout, I hear him. I hear him inside, not outside. Bradek! Bradek! the shout say. Forgive me! I can't keep going, my spirit leave now!

That voice! I don't hear that voice in long time. That voice, him the voice of Berangu. Mother Berangu, where are you? Oh, Mother Berangu, how I love you! Where are you?

I don't hear any more. I know that Berangu call to me as she die. Where she die, I don't know. Another trouble for poor Bradek. I lose my Jinggaya. I lose my Berangu. I don't know where my children are, whether they live or die. All the comfort that Goanna Rock give me don't stop me feel sad that day. I see my tears fall on that rock and soak into his dust.

My children not in this country, so I walk up to Guringbadawah country, up to lake in north. I happy see all that mob up there. I don't see any white feller. I don't see any pox. That mob all same like before. They greet me like friend.

My first question about my children. They say they don't see any children belong my old mob long time. Monanggu, Nawngnaw, where are you? My heart hurt as they take me to Cabba's dad.

Cabba's dad look old. He not so old, but he look old. He look tired. He lie by his fire when I get there. He half get up. "I proper glad see you, nephew," he say. But I see he still got sadness in his eye.

I squat by him. "I glad see you, uncle."

"You hear Berangu?" he ask.

"You hear her too? Yes, I hear her. You know where she is?"

"No. She long way off, that for sure."

"Any of our old mob here?"

"We got three of us here, that all." He tell me about the others. They old women, too old for children. "Them white feller just about finish our mob. Nothing left for old feller like me now."

"I see some of our feller run off into bush, same like me ..."

"If they live, they don't come here. Maybe they keep run other place. But I think maybe they all dead. Soon all our mob dead, none left."

"Oh, uncle, I got two children still. Mother Berangu save them."

"They with your woman?"

"No, uncle. My woman dead. My children, I don't know where they are. Maybe they dead ..."

He quiet a bit. Then he say, "Nephew, you stay here now, you come in with these Guring-badawah?"

I see he want this bad. Don't know how tell him. I say, "Uncle, I like that good. But my children, they out there somewhere. I got to find them children if they alive. I promise Jinggaya I find them children."

He sign he understand. Them eyes sad and empty.

*

Again I don't tell you all that happen. I go back to north and west country, look for my children. I look all over that country, ask every new place if they see any orphan girl and orphan boy in that place. Many seasons come and go. I see more places like that place with that Captain. I see more of them white feller places. I meet some of them white feller not so bad, do some things for white feller, look after sheep and cow same like other black feller, get beef and tea same like other black feller. I try that grog; don't like him! They call me stockman. Stockman not so bad, I track them sheep and cow good, I find them when they go off in bush, bring them back for white feller. I do this many places, all over this country. I learn some of that white feller lingo. When I work for white feller, I got to wear his clothes, got to wear his shirt and his trousers and his hat. Them shirt and trousers no good. Soon as I leave white feller place, I throw off them shirt and trousers. Keep that hat; that hat not bad, keep sun off. I go all over that country year after year, but I don't see my children.

After all them years I come to another of them camp near white feller place. When I come to one of them camp, first thing I do is walk round ask about my children. So I walk round this camp, fire place to fire place, ask about my children. I come to new fire place. One feller squat by this fire. He got long beard like mine get now. I look at him. Do I know him?

He look at me. I see him look at me like he try remember me but can't. I look at him. I sure I know him. He see me look. He stand up.

"I Maulan," he say.

"Maulan! Maulan! Of course! How I glad see you! Look, don't you see who here? I Bradek! That Bradek whose life you save!"

He look me good, then his face get smile that warm my heart. He run up and throw his arms round me. 'Bradek! Bradek, my brother! You live! You got long beard! He got some grey in him, I don't know you! How happy see you! I look out for you all this time!"

We hold on to each other. "You look out for me?" I say. "I look out for you when go back that time too, but don't see."

"No, no, them white feller make us move on. But that not what I mean. I look out for you all this time, because you tell me you lose your children! I know where them children are!"

Do I hear this? I push him to length of arm so I can see his face. Yes, he that Maulan. He got grey in his beard too. He got no nose bone but I know that face and I know this man I trust. "You know where they are?" I don't believe this. "You know? Where? How?"

"Not far, not far! Listen. I tell you. When them white feller make us move on, I come up here with what left of our mob. We come to this place here. Plenty black feller here, work for white feller, live on white feller tucker. We do same. We here long time. I sit at this fire one evening, when I see old woman come out of that bush over there. Yes, right there! That woman, she got two small children with her. She stand over there, at edge of bush, look proper scared. I think, this woman got two small children walk about long time. Soon as I see her, I think of you. I stand up, call out to her, 'Mother,

246

you need help?' She don't answer, but she take two steps toward me, and I see she proper weak and she walk lame. I remember, you say your mother walk with limp! I say to her, 'Mother, Mother, you Mother of Bradek?'

"You got to see her face when I say your name. You see her face, you be proud feller make a face look like that when your name said. She just say, 'Bradek!' then fall to ground. Them children run out round her, start cry. I go over to her. She proper thin, she don't eat much long time. Them children proper thin too, I see they not got long on this earth if they don't eat soon.

"I pick up that Mother, and I see her spirit leaving her. I carry her to fire. She ask how I know Bradek, I say you camp at my fire one time. She say she think you dead, she think your woman dead. She see all them white feller kill your mob dead in your country, she run with them children to what she call Nose Bone country, but she see more white feller there so she run this way. She say she hide her tracks, leave no trail so no white feller can follow.

"Oh, Bradek, I sad tell you this. Your Mother die on this spot, just there. She use all her strength save them children, keep them safe, bring them here to me. Maybe she got to die before, only live long enough do this good thing. Oh Bradek, you got good Mother there! She bring them children right to this camp, right to camp where you got good friend who look after them children! How she know I your friend so bring them to me, I don't

247

know. But that what happen all right.

"I know I no good for look after small child. I bring my own boy to this camp, I know I can't look after him good. But them white feller got a place called Mission up the track, him a place take them children. White feller in that place give children good tucker, look after them good all the time. My own boy in that place, I go see him every week. So I take your children up to Mission, tell them feller there they orphan. They take them children in all right. And them children live there ever since. They still there now!"

I still hold that Maulan at length of arm. Now I pull him to me and hug him. "Maulan! You best friend a feller ever have! Where this Mission? Where?"

He laugh. "Come with me now! Less than one day walk!" Then he stop, and smile leave his face. He look me eye to eye like close friend. He say, "Don't expect too much. They been in that Mission long time now, they don't know our ways. Even my own son, I see him many time but he don't know much of our mob way. They learn way of them white feller."

*

So now you know. This how I find you. Yes, Mary, you my Monanggu and yes, William, you my own Nawngnaw. Now you know how you come to live in Mission. I so happy the day I walk in here! I know you soon as I see you, even though you so big now! I see you proper surprised this hairy feller walk up say he your dad! But now you know, I so happy. You know about your dad and you know about your beautiful mum too. That mum of yours, she best mum any child ever get.

I know you don't come away with me. I see your life not like my life. You forget your lingo, you only got that white feller lingo now. You don't know about live with mob, live in bush. I see that. I see them white feller teach you all sorts of stuff them white feller know. That good, them white feller know a lot of stuff. A lot they don't know, too, don't you forget that. A lot of us black feller know stuff them white feller don't know.

I know I tell you some secret of our mob. You know this against law of our mob, tell you those secrets. But you don't ever learn them secret in your life now. I think I got to tell you them secret, so you know a bit about your mob. You got to understand a bit about your own mob. Plenty more secret I don't tell you.

I got to go back now. I got to go to that ridge where your mum lie, tell her I keep my promise. Her spirit rest good when I tell her that. I got to go back to Goanna Rock too. I belong that place. I know Cabba's dad die. I feel this a while back. When he die, I know maybe I the last of our mob live that old life. You got to live new life, you can't learn them old ways now. I got to live old way. Maybe I go up to that lake in north too. Got to help rest that spirit of Cabba's dad. Take long time for rest that spirit, he great man. I think maybe Cabba's dad leave The Bone there for me.

I so happy find you. I happy know you live. More happy know I keep my promise to Jinggaya. Now I keep my promise, not got to search no more. Now I can go join that woman I love more than anything. I go back to Goanna Rock, I sit on that rock, paint that sign up good, sing good! Bradek only Goanna left know where that sacred board hid! When I hide him last time, no man ever find him again! Who look after Goanna Rock when I die? Who make ceremony, rest my spirit when I die? I die at Goanna Rock, maybe my spirit never rest. But still I go back to Goanna Rock. Yes, I go back to Goanna Rock, sit on that rock a happy man, happy know my children alive, happy I keep my promise, happiest of all sit there, look over my country and wait join Jinggaya!

Look, Monanggu! Look, Nawngnaw! See over there, over the lake, one white cockatoo fly round in the sunset? Don't he squawk! He call to his friends in them trees. Look! See them feller come out of them trees? Yes, they all fly up to him. Look! More and more of them cockatoo come out of them trees. They fly round and round in big circle. Every cockatoo in this country got to be in that circle! So many they black out the sky. And they all squawk and squawk! You know what they say when they do that? They say, 'We are the cockatoos! We own this land! All this land is our land! You other feller, keep out! Keep out!"